Bighorn Gold

Jesper Tubbs has spent his life wandering the western mountains searching for the elusive glint of gold. But Fate plays its fickle hand late in his life when, at the point of starvation, he literally stumbles upon a fabulous strike.

But Tubbs finds far more than just gold. His chance discovery is to turn sane men into wanton killers who will stop at nothing to find his secret location deep in the Tobacco Root Mountains, and claim it as their own.

Bighorn Gold

Art Isberg

A Black Horse Western

ROBERT HALE

© Art Isberg 2019
First published in Great Britain 2019

ISBN 978-0-7198-2879-9

The Crowood Press
The Stable Block
Crowood Lane
Ramsbury
Marlborough
Wiltshire SN8 2HR

www.bhwesterns.com

Robert Hale is an imprint
of The Crowood Press

Typeset by
Derek Doyle & Associates, Shaw Heath
Printed and bound in Great Britain by
4Bind Ltd, Stevenage, SG1 2XT

ONE

Jesper Tubbs had to stop climbing in the shadows of that late afternoon canyon. Going down on his knees, he grabbed the old rifle barrel with both hands and lowered his head on his arms. The gnawing pain of hunger in his shrunken stomach was crippling. His meagre grub stake of food had completely run out nearly ten days ago. He'd been reduced to drinking pine tea, eating plant roots and tree squirrels, when he could catch one of the little rodents he'd set snares for. Tubbs, already a thin man by nature, had grown so skinny that every time he tightened his belt another notch it felt like it was grating on his backbone. His bearded face held two dark hollows that were eyes. His clothes were torn and patched, his boots worn down to stitching. Jesper Tubbs was slowly starving to death, whether he knew it or not. Yet he would not quit prospecting for gold. He'd die trying.

Back as his small camp higher up the mountain, a simple canvas lean-to tied over poles served as his only shelter. A worn steel pick, shovel and gold pan leaned against a tree in front of a cold fire pit. Tethered to a tree stood his only friend and companion, a big-eared mule named Jenny. Tubbs had to get back there now and lay down to rest. He'd wandered, dug and panned his way through these Tobacco Root Mountains for five long months, not to mention a lifetime of prospecting other wild country without ever making a gold strike. It was a disease without cure once it clouded the mind and left only one goal in life.

Earlier, far below, his hopes had been ignited finding a glint of flour gold while panning in a small creek. He'd carefully followed that trail up, trying to find the source of colour, but without success. Out of food and luck, he'd gone out hunting again with his old, single-shot rifle, praying desperately to find any kind of game. As the afternoon sun sank behind high peaks surrounding him, that too had failed. A lesser man, or a saner one, would have quit and saved himself, leaving this godforsaken country to try to reach help, but not Jesper Tubbs. Back in civilization, people would say a man like him was 'bushed', which meant out of his mind, half mad, searching aimlessly for a golden promise that never materialized until he died a slow, miserable death alone.

When Jesper opened his eyes to prepare to pull himself up to his feet, long shadows of evening already sent misty fingers shrouding the mountains around him. Gripping the rifle, he started to stand but stopped, eyes suddenly riveted on a rocky ridge along the skyline only forty yards above. There, as if by magic, stood a golden Bighorn ram, big, drenched in the final rays of setting sun, surveying his lofty domain. Jesper couldn't believe his eyes. They must be playing tricks on him. He slowly sank down on his knees, rubbing his eyes trying to clear them. When he dared look up again, the golden ram was still there. Slowly, with trembling hands, he began cranking the hammer back on the old long gun, never taking his eyes off the ram. That big, wild sheep carried enough meat on him to last Jesper weeks. He could stay in the mountains even longer continuing his search for gold. All he had to do was make that one shot count.

With aching arms, he lifted the rifle to his shoulder. The front blade sight wobbled on and off the ram. He tried desperately to steady it. Suddenly, the ram swung his massive, full curled head to look downhill into the shadows where Jesper knelt. Had some small sound or movement alerted him? The ram stiffened, ready to run. Tubbs had to shoot now. The front sight swung back on the ram. Jesper pulled the trigger to a roar and cloud of black powder ignition, obscuring the sight of the animal for several moments.

When it cleared, the golden ram had disappeared. Had he missed the only chance he had to survive? Crawling on his hands and knees, he climbed for the ridge. Reaching it, gasping out of breath, he peered into gloomy shadows down the other side. There, not fifteen feet away, lay the dead body of the great ram. Tubbs got to his feet and stumbled down to the animal, dropping to his knees and placing both hands on its still warm body. Tears of joy ran down his sunken cheeks. He might not find gold this day, but he had something just as valuable. He had food!

When he'd composed himself, he gathered some wood and started a small fire before gutting the sheep, slicing off strips of mountain mutton and roasting them over the flames. He gorged himself until he felt sick to his stomach. Night had fallen. Stars came out, blazing icy white. But Tubbs was not about to abandon his heaven-sent ram to bears, wolves or coyotes. He decided to spend the night right here protecting his kill. Lying down between the ram and fire, he fed small sticks into the flames, until falling into exhausted sleep.

In the icy dawn, last night's fire was reduced to a pile of cold white ashes. Jesper, rolled up in a ball, stirred to the cold, but did not move. His stomach was still in revolt, the cobwebs of sleep clouding his mind, only vaguely aware something wasn't right. Strange sounds assaulted his ears, screeching sounds and squawks right in his face. He felt the sudden stab of a sharp beak in his chest, cutting through his threadbare shirt. Opening his eyes, he screamed in horror, flailing wildly at half a dozen black-hooded vultures sitting on him and the ram. Staggering to his feet, he screamed and kicked as the red-eyed birds vaulted into the air. They had taken him for dead just like the ram they'd been feeding on. When the shakes finally subsided, he dabbed at the bloody spots on his shirt, before sitting back down to try to think clearly about what to do next.

He began by rolling the carcass over to start skinning the entire ram, preparing to quarter it for Jenny to haul back to camp. He suddenly stopped, leaning closer.

The ground was covered in dried blood from the animal, but something else was there. He wiped it away with his hand. Down on his hands and knees, he squinted harder. It was a lace-like pattern of pure white quartz, interspersed with veins of gold. He dug faster with bare hands, clearing off more scree, exposing more golden threads. Jesper couldn't help himself. He threw his head back and howled out loud, still not believing what his eyes told him was right there. After years of searching, privation and shattered dreams, the Red Gods of Hunt had dropped the great ram exactly on this spot for him to find. It could only be a feat that was heaven-sent. There could be no other explanation for it!

All that day Tubbs worked. He brought Jenny down to the kill site and roped thick quarters on her, before climbing back up to camp and hanging the meat in the cool shade of a tall pine tree near his lean-to. He cut off small strips, hanging them to air-dry into jerky, before hanging the great, curly horned head in the same tree. Bone-tired by late that afternoon, he wanted to get back down to the quartz vein, but was too exhausted to do so. He had to begin thinking even more carefully now about his amazing discovery. He would eventually have to take whatever ore he could dig up with pick and shovel to have it assayed in the town of Eagle Buttes, over a week's ride away. How could he keep that secret from the prying eyes and ears of greedy men? Wherever gold is found, he knew that deadly combination always followed.

That night, by a crackling fire, he ate the ram's entire

liver for dinner, then smoked a pipe full of root tobacco, from which the mountains around him were named. Sooner or later he'd have to go in for supplies, too. Jesper Tubbs was about to become a very rich man. He was ready for it, but not the consequences. The first thing he decided not to do was file a claim on his fabulous strike. That would only expose its location to other men. It would be weeks before he made that first long trip into town. He needed more time to think things through to protect his hidden bonanza.

With renewed strength, Tubbs worked like a man possessed each day, riding early down to the golden ridge and hammering out more quartz, filling two large canvas bags. Back at camp, he laboriously crushed the quartz even further with his sledgehammer, reducing it further. He dumped the quartz-only pieces into a pile of snow white pebbles that grew in size each day. After two weeks of hard labour, the pile stood nearly three feet tall and as big around. Now his original dilemma came back to haunt him. He had to have his gold refined further and assayed at the stamp mill in Eagle Buttes. There was no way to get around it. Maybe on the long ride in he could finally come up with some answers to protect his secret find as much as possible.

Tubbs had just finished packing the heavy bags on Jenny when he saw a line of riders slowly coming down through timber toward his camp. By the flash of colour of their ponies, he knew it had to be a party of Shoshone Indians that called these Tobacco Root Mountains their home. They tolerated the old man, thinking he must be crazy to always be wandering around and breaking up rocks with his hammer, and living in his meagre camp against the elements. Standing Bear, the chief, rode in the lead. Reaching the small clearing, he pulled his horse to a stop. Jesper raised his hand in greeting, forcing a smile, while the chief's dark eyes took in the camp, then fell on the pile of crushed white quartz.

Jesper always noted the proud way the Shoshones carried themselves, dressed in hand-stitched buckskin clothes, leather leggings and knee-high moccasin boots. Their long, black hair was often braided down one side or hung at the back with an eagle feather, their necks adorned with necklaces of coloured beads or metal amulets. Standing Bear offered no greeting. Easing down off his horse, he walked directly to the pile of glistening white quartz, staring down on it. Clearly it had caught his fancy, but the expression on his face said he was puzzled what it might be for. Jesper immediately understood that look.

'This is just some rocks I've been hammering on,' he tried a quick explanation, shrugging his shoulders to imply it meant little to him. Standing Bear ignored him. Leaning down he scooped up a handful of quartz, letting it slowly trickle down through his fingers. He liked the look and feel of it, before looking up at Tubbs.

'Why . . . you . . . do this?' he asked in broken English.

'Oh, I just like to see what's inside them, that's all. You know I always like to have a big bag of rocks around to hammer on. It don't mean nothing more than that.'

The chief turned to one of his braves. Pointing to the

pile, he issued a brief order. The Indian quickly slid off his horse, retrieving a leather satchel from Standing Bear's horse, filling it to the top. The chief's eyes went to Jenny, loaded and ready to leave.

'You go?' he questioned.

'Yes, I'm going to town for supplies. I won't be gone too long. Staying around lots of white people always brings trouble, but you already know that.'

'No bring . . . white man . . . back here. Come alone.'

'You don't have to worry none about that. I don't want them here anymore than you do. I always live alone. You've seen me. You know I speak the truth.'

Standing Bear stared at Tubbs a moment longer, and once more time at the pile of quartz, before turning for his horse. Tubbs lifted a hand in goodbye, watching the line of Indians turn their horses around and start back up the ridge until they slowly became lost in thick timber. He breathed a sigh of relief, and for good reason. He could never really be certain what the Shoshone chief was thinking or might do. His facial expression rarely changed, his dark eyes and stoic stare always scrutinizing him for some sign of false word or deed.

He always found it best to play the innocent, just a harmless, crazy old man wandering the mountains talking to himself. Now, more than ever, he had to continue that act with his sudden discovery of the golden ledge just down from camp. To do otherwise could mean the chief would order him out of the mountains and for good, with the promise of death should he return.

Eagle Buttes lay over a week's journey away far across the Tobacco Root Mountains, down in a small valley ringed by high peaks. Jesper led the loaded Jenny on foot, starting out soon as the Shoshones were out of sight. It was time to begin his dangerous brush with civilization and people asking too many questions. One of the great pleasures of living alone as he did for so many years was that he didn't have to explain what he was doing and where he was doing it to anyone else. Solitude was the welcome barrier that meant safety and peace of mind. Now all that was at risk, yet he had no other choice. Only the six stamp mill at the edge of town could process his precious ore and take it through the mercury amalgamation process needed to produce pure gold and the real worth of his find. It was a chance he had to take.

Richmond Tyrell Sturgis was a man of considerable wealth and influence in Eagle Buttes. He had not only helped lay out the lots forming the new town years earlier, but he had sold the lots or rented them to businesses that came to the new town hoping to prosper. The original reason for the town's existence was an unlimited supply of tall timber that could be harvested, milled then shipped by wagon miles downhill into the flatlands for much-needed construction material. Some mining for both gold and silver also spurred early development, and the addition of the stamp mill. Several hard rock mines had originally been opened, but only a single one now remained to make any profit; the Bladesdale Mine owned by Lewis Bladesdale and his twin brother, Dean. The early thinking that this area would be another big bonanza quickly faded away, although rumours still persisted that the real mother lode in the Tobacco Root Mountains had never been found. Wylie Lee, owner of the stamp mill, processed all the Bladesdale ore and lesser amounts of several smaller operations farther south that had to be wagon-hauled to his stamp mill.

Sturgis had his financial hand in almost every business venture in town. He'd also been elected mayor twice, and had a controlling interest in the town's one and only bank, the Evergreen Mercantile. There was precious little that went on in Eagle Buttes that he did not know about or have his financial hand in. To solidify his position further, he hired his close friend Cas Wickman as sheriff, who regularly reported to the Eagle Buttes Citizen Committee about current goings on, a committee Sturgis also headed. Wickman's position assured that his pal and benefactor kept his hands clean of any scandal or questions of impropriety in business dealings that might arise. R.T. Sturgis had his own little empire neatly tucked away in his tailored vest pocket, along with his hundred dollar gold watch and fancy linked chain. Like most men of unlimited power, he used it as he pleased without regret or conscience. Sturgis never wore a badge nor needed to. Everyone in town knew he was the real law, or paid the price for their ignorance sooner or later.

Jesper, leading Jenny, pulled to a stop at the edge of timber after his long trek out of the mountains, looking down on Eagle Buttes. A rust-coloured sky said sundown was only minutes away. His timing was not by accident. Tubbs wanted to use the cover of darkness to draw as little attention to himself as possible, and fewer questions. Most people in town knew who he was, even though his visits were infrequent and only to buy supplies, then he would disappear for months on end again. Like the Shoshone Indians, they simply thought he was a strange loner living out his life deep in the mountains on a wild goose chase after gold that didn't exist. If anyone knew what the packs on Jenny's back contained it would start another instant gold rush. Jesper pulled at his beard before deciding to skirt town and stay out of sight by moving at the edge of the timber, until reaching Lee's stamp mill. He confided his plan to his long-time friend.

'You know, old girl, everyone thinks you're just a twenty-dollar mule, but they don't know you could be carrying a thousand dollars worth of gold ore on your back! Let's get on to Lee's place. We both can use a good feed and rest.'

Wylie Lee was in his shack next to the stamp mill, cooking dinner. He'd shut down the water supply that drove the endless roar of heavy, metal stamps crushing rough ore down into crumbling pieces. Even in dead silence, the constant ringing in his ears never stopped. The slamming, mill hammers had rendered Lee nearly deaf. He didn't hear the first knock on the door either, until Jesper pounded it harder a second and third time. Crossing the room, he opened the door to the soft glow on his coal oil lamp, lighting Tubbs' face. It took Lee a

15

moment to actually realize who it was. He leaned even closer.

'Well, I'll be damned. Jesper Tubbs, is that you? What are you doin' back in town as this hour? I haven't seen you in a coon's age!'

'Hello, Wylie. Yeah it's me, all right. I need a place to stay for the night, for me and my mule. Tomorrow I want you to run some ore for me.'

'Run ore, where did you get anything worth runnin'? You find another dry hole, someplace?' He snickered, a yellow-toothed smile through several missing teeth.

'Never you mind where I got it. All I need is for you to run it, and keep whatever comes of it to your own self. Now how about someplace we can bed down?'

Lee let his unexpected guest spend the night in a small shack he used to keep spare mill parts in. Jenny was hobbled nearby to feed on lush greenery near the stream that fed the stamp mill. Early next morning, Jesper was up at the first hint of dawn. Tired as he was from his long hike out of the mountains, he'd slept little, thinking about what today could bring. He pounded on Lee's door again, rousting him out of bed, much to his displeasure.

'You only got two leather satchels to run through?' He sat on the edge of the bunk scratching his head, scowling at the old man. 'What's the big rush? I ain't even had time to put on a pot of coffee, so I can see straight. Why don't we wait until Bladesdale brings in a load from his diggins'? They're due in here about today. That way it won't cost you as much if I run the mill all day long.'

'I don't have time for that. I'll pay you whatever I have to just to run my own goods. Let's get to it. Then I can buy some supplies and get out of town. Too many people make me nervous.'

Lee still grumbled to himself while getting dressed and going outside, opening the water gate that started the heavy stamps working up and down. When the ringing began, both men lugged the two, heavy leather bags to the mill race, dumping them into the feed box. Jesper stood back watching his ore being crushed into tiny pieces, praying silently to himself the outcome would be as rich as he'd hoped. When both loads had been completely pulverized and processed through, Wylie transferred them into a large, rotating metal pan where the ore swirled with a mix of mercury and water, the mercury trapping gold in its shiny embrace. After another thorough mixing, the water along with the mercury was boiled off, leaving pure gold. The sudden look of astonishment on Wylie's face spoke volumes even before he could clear his throat to speak.

'Well, what about it? How rich is it?' Jesper's eyes already gleamed with satisfaction.

Lee took in a breath, stepping back. 'You have to understand . . . all I can do is give you a rough estimate, from what little you brought in. I usually figure this by the ton, for hard rock mining.'

'I understand that. Give me your best estimate, anyway.'

'If anything else you bring in here yields what this does . . . I'd have to say you're getting over twice as much as the Bladesdales are. They're getting about one troy ounce of gold per ton. I guess I'd also have to admit, this is the richest ore sample I've ever put through my stamps.'

Jesper felt a shiver of excitement course through his body. He knew all along his chance discovery had to be special, but not this special. After all the years searching, living on practically nothing, praying he'd make it another day to find that mother lode, the Tobacco Root Mountains had made his wild dream come true. He took in a deep breath before speaking.

'I'll pay you whatever I owe you out of this ore. But you keep this under your hat, you understand? This ain't no one else's business but my own. I expect you to honour that, you hear?'

'Listen, Tubbs. You won't keep a strike like this quiet for very long. You gotta' know word will get out whether I say it nor not. You just going into town buying supplies and paying for it with this gold will start everyone talking. You can't stop that.'

'Maybe, but I'll be long gone before any of it starts. Right now I want you to keep your lip buttoned. That's all I'm asking.'

This time Wylie Lee didn't answer. Looking down at the gold Jesper poured into his hand, he was certain Eagle Buttes was about to explode with questions without answers about the sudden gold strike. He glanced back up at Tubbs with some final advice.

'You'd better ride fast and far, if you think you can outrun news like this. Good luck, Jesper. You're gonna' need it!'

TWO

R.T. Sturgis was sitting at the desk in his office when Sirius Weems, owner of one of the dry goods stores in town, came in. R.T. looked up from the papers he was reading, wondering why Weems was here at all. He wasn't due to make a payment on the lot he'd purchased for another two weeks.

'Hello, Mr Sturgis. I hope I'm not interrupting anything important.' Weems approached the desk, hat in hand.

'Nothing I can't get back to.' Sturgis eyed him curiously. 'What brings you here now?'

'Well . . . I had a very unusual transaction with a man at my store today. I believe his name is Jesper Tubbs. Do you know him?'

'I know of him. He's an old coot who a lot of people around here think is half crazy. I'm told he lives someplace back in the mountains, like a hermit. They say he's a prospector, always looking for gold, the poor fool. What about him?'

'I guess he may be half touched in the head, but he

came into my store and bought two hundred dollars' worth of supplies and dried food. He paid for it with this.'

Weems untied the drawstrings on top of a small leather pouch, pouring out a silver dollar-sized pile of pure gold. 'Maybe he isn't half as crazy as people think?'

Sturgis's eyes locked on the gold and he came to his feet. 'Is he still here in town?'

'I don't know. He left my place most of an hour ago. I didn't watch which way he went. I was too surprised to.'

'Why didn't you come here sooner and let me know about this?' R.T.'s voice suddenly turned darker.

'I had to get someone to watch the store. My wife's out of town visiting her sister down in Winters. It took me a little while to get help.'

Sturgis brushed by Weems, exiting his office into a larger parlour room where Sheriff Cass Wickman and two other men were sitting at a table casually playing cards.

'Cas, you Hoyt and Jury get off your butts, and go get me Wylie Lee. Bring him back here even if you have to drag him. After that, saddle up and go after that old man, Jesper Tubbs. You know, the one who comes to town once in a while on a mule. He was just at Weems' place buying goods. He can't be that far away. You should be able to ride him down pretty fast. Bring him back here and don't come back until you do. Now get moving!'

Jesper normally walked and led Jenny wherever they went, even if she was unloaded, but not this time. She was as big as a horse and sturdy strong from all her years doing mountain work. Her long, white-tipped nose, big floppy ears pitched forward and dark brown body accentuated by a coal black tail that hung nearly to the ground made her a sight to behold. It also made her something else. In the timber and shadows of high country, she blended in perfectly. Jesper knew he had to move fast. Wylie's words still rung in his ears. He rode on top of the supplies and urged Jenny up onto the dim game trail they'd used coming to town. Men would be coming after him. He was certain of it. Leaning now, he began talking to Jenny, urging her higher, faster, without let-up.

'Come on, ol' girl. Dig them strong legs in and don't stop. We've got to make tracks, and I don't mean maybe. Trouble is on the way for sure, and we can't let them catch up no matter what. Once we reach rocky ground, we'll be all right. They can't track us there. Giddy up, now!'

R.T. Sturgis stood with hands on his hips, staring down on Wylie Lee, sitting slouched over in his office chair. Lee knew what was coming and why he was here. If looks could kill, he'd already be a goner.

'Why didn't you get yourself over here and tell me about this find of Tubbs'?' R.T. demanded. 'Instead, I have to send Cas to drag you here. You know that property your mill is on, don't you?' Lee nodded but did not look up. 'I could take it back in a minute and there isn't a damn thing you could do about it. You'd end up right back in the weeds, where you used to be.'

Lee finally summoned the courage to speak up. 'Listen, I was gonna' tell you . . . only Tubbs asked me not to tell anyone. At least not for a little while.'

'Not to tell anyone? I own this town and everyone in it. I made it by the sweat off my back and my own money. I expect to be told anything important, and that goes for anyone who thinks he's hit the jackpot with some mining claim. Are you so thick-headed I have to explain that to you? Now I want to know everything he told you, every damn word of it, and how rich this ore of his was, and I mean right now!'

Wylie took in a slow breath, trying to compose himself. 'He told me he ain't gonna' file no claim, so no one knows the location. From what little he brought to town, I'd have to say his ore is a whole lot better even than the Bladesdale mine. It's the richest I've ever run. The old man must have hit the mother lode jackpot, someplace back in them mountains where some people thought there had to be a bonanza. He must be on it, big time.'

'Did he give you any hint how far away it is?'

'No, but it must be a hard rock vein he's working, not a placer creek or stream. It's all in white quartz, and that means only one man has to hammer it out a piece at a time with pick and shovel. To really work somethin' like that he'd have to have more men, heavy equipment and supplies, maybe even drive through a road to bring it all out. What Tubbs had was just what he could haul on that mule of his.'

Sturgis turned away, jaws clenched, shaking his head, cussing under his breath. 'If my men don't run him down, and he shows up at your place again, you better get yourself over here and let me know about it, and I mean real fast. You let him slip away like that again and you'll wish you were never born. Now get out of here before I lose my temper and throw you out!'

Cas Wickman rode in the lead, savagely spurring his horse higher, the struggling animal slipping and sliding over soft ground up the steep timbered slope. Hoyt and Jury fell further behind trying to keep up. After nearly an hour trying to close the distance on Tubbs without ever catching even a glimpse of him, Cas yanked his sweat-soaked animal to a halt on a small level spot. Getting down, he shielded his eyes with both hands against the glare of sun, squinting higher up the mountain. Nothing moved save the distant flash of a blue jay's wings coasting across the canyon.

'If we're even still on the trail, this Tubbs must be riding Winged Pegasus,' the sheriff, exclaimed taking off his hat and wiping off hot sweat running down his face with the back of his shirt sleeve, as Jury and Hoyt caught up.

'I don't know who Winged Pegasus is, but I don't see how any old man on a mule could outclimb all three of us?' Hoyt shook his head, untying the canteen off his horse and taking a long pull at the spout, as Jury came up beside him.

'I'll tell you one more thing right now. I ain't about to kill my horse going any higher. This is as far as I'm going. We must have lost his tracks someplace back down in timber. No one is any higher up this mountain than we are . . . no one.'

Wickman didn't answer for a moment. He remembered Sturgis's order not to come back without the old man, but there was nothing else left to do. He grimaced, rubbing the back of his neck, letting out a long sigh. 'I guess the best we can do now is give these horses a good blow, then start back down. You know there'll be hell to pay when we get back, don't you two?'

'Then tell him to saddle up and give it a try, himself,' Jury shot back. 'We may as well be chasing a ghost, instead of some crackpot old man on a mule. He must be crazy to live up here, anyway!'

On a rocky outcrop far above covered in a thick stand of white-barked quaking aspen, Jesper leaned low across Jenny's back, peeking through limbs at the tiny images of three riders below. He was tickled, chuckling under his breath, watching the riders saddle up to begin winding their way back down the mountain. Reaching forward, he grabbed Jenny by one of her long ears, bending it back.

'Well, ol' girl, you left them flatlanders so far behind they're likely talking to themselves about it. Their horses can't hold a candle to you when it comes to mountain climbing. Now all we have to do is cross over the top and take the ridge to the next canyon and start back for home. When we get there I'm gonna' fix us a big feed of beans and fatback. It's one of my favourite meals and I know it's yours, too. From here on we'll just take our sweet time. We're back in our country now, not with them city folks. Come on ol' girl, let's go home.'

*

Sturgis had become so obsessed over the location of Jesper's hidden gold strike, he spent most of the next two weeks either pacing the floor in his office or studying maps of surrounding mountains, often with huge blank spots on them because no white man had ever been in those areas. For a man like R.T. used to getting whatever he wanted with only the snap of his fingers, or his initials hastily scrawled on a piece of paper, his failure was maddening. He had everything a man could want: wealth, political power, grudging respect, even the law on his side when he ordered it. And yet, a broken down old hermit sitting on a fortune in gold, someplace back in wild country with a flop-eared mule, had completely outfoxed him. Something else that worried him even more was the thought that if Tubbs ever did develop his gold strike to full-scale mining, he might end up even richer than he was. It drove Sturgis to the point he began drinking heavily, something he'd largely avoided most of his life.

Occasional visitors to his office for business matters always ended up with R.T. turning the conversation into any ideas they might have about exactly where Tubbs might be holed up. No one had any more ideas than he did, until one day when he called Cas, Hoyt and Jury into his office to go over the whole story again. He wanted to know again exactly the point where they'd lost the trail that day going after the old man.

'Like I said, he was going straight uphill toward the Tobacco Roots, but we never found out how far.' Wickman retold the tale. 'A man could get lost in that wilderness country without even trying. Maybe we lost the trail and were in the wrong spot. I don't know for sure, but never got close enough to see him, and we tried plenty hard.'

Sturgis sat at his desk, resting his chin on both hands with his eyes closed, thinking the whole thing over for the hundredth time. Across from him, Hoyt slowly rolled a cigarette, lit it, blowing out a long stream of smoke. He didn't add anything to the conversation. He was tired of talking about it.

'One thing for sure is, wherever he goes, it's a long, long way away from town,' Cas added. 'Didn't Weems say he bought over two hundred dollars worth of supplies? That tells me he means to stay back in there for months before he comes back out again. And I know one other thing, too. You could put an army in those mountains and never find him.'

Sturgis opened his eyes, suddenly pounding on the desk. 'There has to be some way to find him, damn it. Don't sit there and tell me I can't!'

'There might be ... someone who knows where he is,' Jury unrepentantly spoke up, his pals eyeing him in surprise.

'What, who?' R.T. shot back. 'Tell me what you're talking about?'

'The Shoshone Indians. All that high country back there is their own stamping grounds. Even the army stays out of it, or has to go to war with them. I'd bet a hundred dollar horse they know where Tubbs is holed up. They don't trust any white men and never come close here. I think their chief is named Standing Bear, or something like that.'

'How do you know any of this is a fact, and not some wild tale?' Sturgis got up and came around the desk, facing Jury. 'Explain that.'

'My cousin Darrell Pickett rides with the US Cavalry under the command of George Crook. Last time I saw him he told me Standing Bear wouldn't be put on a reservation. He broke off talks with half his tribe and a bunch of young bucks ready to fight to keep their freedom. They went to the Crow Indians to ask them to join up against the cavalry, but they refused. That's when Standing Bear took his people and headed into the Tobacco Root Mountains to hole up. He's been there ever since.'

'If everything you say is true, how does any white man get to this Standing Bear to ask about Tubbs?'

'No white man can, but maybe through the Crows. They likely know where he is and Tubbs, too.'

'Do you believe the Crows would actually do something like that?'

'I don't know that for sure, but there's only one way to find out.'

Sturgis didn't answer for a moment. His mind was running wild with the sudden, new idea of Jury's. Wickman looked over at Hoyt with the same surprise on his face. Jury was about the last person he expected to come up with anything that made sense, yet he had obviously gotten R.T.'s attention and fast. Cas always thought of Jury as much more a loner who kept his thoughts to himself. Sturgis hired him for his fast gun and the willingness to use it without question. Now the boss might see him in a different light. Cas decided to

27

do a little questioning on his own, taking the play away from Jury.

'Why didn't you say something about this idea of yours before now?'

'You never asked me. Neither did anyone else.'

Cas started to respond, but Sturgis cut him off. 'I want to know how we can contact these Crows you're talking about. How would that be possible?'

'With guns. You offer them new rifles and cartridges. That's what they want most of all. That's the way to get them to talk.'

R.T. stared hard at Jury, thinking all this over. The more he considered it, the more it seemed to make sense and might actually work. He could feel the excitement of it pounding under his fancy vest.

'The Crow nation is up north from here, isn't it?' he asked.

'Yeah,' Jury nodded. 'I'm told they stay someplace close to Fort Pakston on the Madison River. The cavalry sometimes uses them as scouts. I've never been there, but I heard that's where their main village is.'

'That's got to be over a week's ride from here isn't it?' Wickman questioned. 'And if you tried to get there by wagon, it would be even longer than that. That's a long way to go for something that might not pan out.'

'I don't care how far it is,' Sturgis quickly countered. 'It's the only idea I've heard that might have a chance to work. You didn't come up with anything, did you? I'll get my hands on these rifles, but it won't be easy. Jury, I want you and Hoyt to make the wagon ride up to this fort and find those Crows. Offer them anything you have to, but find out where Tubbs is hiding out.'

'What about me?' Wickman's tone of voice betrayed that he felt he was being left out.

'I want you to stay here in town and keep things in line. Jury and Hoyt can handle this on their own. Jury, you rent a wagon over at Trumbels Livery, while I see how to get these rifles. Get down to Weems dry goods and get enough grub and supplies to make the trip. Tell both of them to put it on my bill. When you get all this lined up, get back here and I'll give you some extra cash in case you need it. Let's get moving on all this. I want you to leave town soon as I come up with those rifles.'

Two days later, in the alley behind Sturgis's office, Jury and Hoyt hefted two heavy cases of new rifles and ammo boxes into the wagon, while R.T. stood with his hands on his hips talking to Wickman.

'I had to lean on a few people to get these new Henry rifles, but once they saw I wasn't going to take no for an answer, they gave them up. They are so new, even the cavalry hasn't seen them yet. If Jury is right about these Crows, it'll all be well worth what I had to pay for them.'

'I don't know,' Wickman shook his head. 'I'd hate to think you spent all that money just because Jury said so. What if he's wrong?'

'I'll worry about that if it happens. Right now this idea of his is all I've got. I'm going to find that old man, come hell or high water. Doing so could literally make me a millionaire. I've got the money and connections to use hard rock mining, no matter how far away it is. Tubbs doesn't. He'll die of old age before he makes any real money bringing ore out two sacks at a time on a mule's back. I'm going to find that strike of his even if I have to kill for it. That's where you might have to come in.'

Cas glanced at R.T. but didn't answer. He knew he was bought and paid for pretending to be the law, Sturgis's law, but killing wasn't something he'd ever had to do before. Locking up some people and threatening others Sturgis wanted out of the way was one thing, killing was something else again. Jury spoke up before he could respond.

'All right, we're loaded up and about ready to go.' He looked up from the wagon bed after tying down a canvas tarp covering the load.

'Here's some extra cash.' Sturgis leaned down, handing him a leather wallet thick with bills. 'Use it if you have to, but don't go spending it if you don't. If you two can pull this off with the Crows, there's an extra hundred dollars in it for each of you.'

Hoyt looked at Jury, a big smile spreading across his whiskered face. 'I'd go to hell and back for an extra hundred!'

Jury levelled a stare at his partner before speaking. 'Don't go spending it too soon. If the Crows turn on us, you might get your wish about seeing hell sooner than you think.'

Fort Pakston was named in honour of cavalry officer William Delaney Pakston, who was killed four years earlier in a deadly ambush by a band of renegade Indians from part of Standing Bear's original tribe before he broke off talks with the military. The log-built fort was the only outpost for whites, soldiers or civilians within sixty miles of any thread of civilization. Constructed on the Madison River, it was originally the meeting site for fur trappers years earlier to barter and trade before building large log rafts and floating downstream until they reached the first white settlements where they could sell off their furs to buyers from Canada and back east.

The army built the isolated fort to have at least one tenuous foothold in the far north close to the Shoshone and Crow tribes if more trouble erupted. The fort's twelve-feet-high walls housed a garrison of cavalry troopers under the new command of Captain Rutherford L. Ryder, one of the youngest men ever to reach that rank. He intended to make a name for himself doing so. Its interior housed a rough barracks for the men, main office and quarters for officers, and a modest kitchen and dining area. A small blacksmith shop was situated near the horse stalls. A pair of guards manned the walkway parapet above a heavy log double gate. Each night the gate was closed and barred until dawn. Ryder didn't trust the Crows, and the feeling was mutual. An unspoken truce always hung in the air.

Cavalry excursions outside the fort were kept to modest distances and lasted little longer than two or sometimes three days at most. In this remote location, Indians from both tribes far outnumbered white soldiers. The fort's existence was mainly to 'show the flag', in hostile country, with the aim of expanding it sometime at some point in the future.

Frank Jury and Delbert Hoyt spent ten long days plodding north in the wagon to reach Pakston. After finding the Madison River, they followed its broad path until midday on the eleventh, when they saw smoke rising above screening pines ahead, and smelled the unmistakable odour of the horse barn. Jury quickly ordered his pal to pull the wagon into a line of trees in a small side canyon, short of the fort's entrance.

'We've got to stash these rifles and ammo boxes someplace out of this wagon. We're not going in there with it loaded in back for some soldier boy to stick his nose into and ask questions. I didn't come this far to end up in no stockade, not for Sturgis or anyone else. Let's get to it.'

One of the blue-uniformed troopers atop the parapet wall eyed the wagon with interest as it rattled toward the front gate. He was surprised to see both men were white. He yelled down to open the gate, while waving the wagoners in. As they passed under him he pointed toward the stables, telling the driver to pull the wagon up over there. Jury twisted in his seat, taking in the sights, sounds and smells of the interior as Hoyt pulled the wagon to a halt. After nearly two weeks of struggle on a winding path that was little more than a faint wheel track, it was a relief to be around people again, even if they all wore uniforms and could be a real danger. Both men stepped down out of the wagon, eyeing each other with satisfaction. The first part of Sturgis's plan was completed. Before either of them could say a word, a tall lanky cavalry officer strode toward them, gold stripes on his sleeve announcing he was a sergeant.

'I'd have to say this is the first wagon I've seen come in here in quite a while, except for our supply wagon, which only makes the trip three times a year. You two took a real chance doing so without a military escort. My name is Sergeant Cleary,' he said, extending his hand.

'It did take some doing.' Jury eyed the sergeant cautiously. 'We kept our eyes open all the way.'

'I'll say you did. What brings you way out here? We don't see many people from the outside?'

'Ah . . . we're traders, looking to sell or trade with the Crows, if we can find them,' Jury answered, never taking his eyes off Cleary to see if his story was working.

'Trade? What do you have to trade with? You might have made a long wagon ride for nothing. The Crows don't have much for trade.'

'We've got cloth, beads, cooking pots and some traps, too. We might even do a little trapping ourselves while we're here. I heard this used to be good country for taking fur.'

'Yes, it used to be, but very few trappers are going to come this far back on their own. That's dangerous business. We've got two Indian tribes that wander most of this land, the Crows and Shoshones. They don't take to whites coming in here trapping their ground. It could be a good way to lose your hair. We have sometimes been able to use the Crows for scouts on marches outside the fort, but they stay pretty much to themselves.'

'Do any of them speak any American?' Hoyt questioned.

'A couple do use a kind of pidgin English. Red Moccasin and Blue Swallow are best at it. I believe they might have picked it up from the last fur trappers who used to come in here.'

'We'd sure like to meet those two so we can talk a little trade,' Jury was quick to respond.

'I can ask them if they'd agree to meet you, but I wouldn't guarantee anything. The Crows have their own way of doing things. They still don't trust whites for a lot of reasons, and that includes us. It took us quite a while just to get them to scout for us. Probably the only reason they did so was for some protection from the Shoshones that live farther back in the mountains. They're the real trouble in this part of the country.'

'If you can get those two you just mentioned to meet with us, we'll give our idea a try,' Jury said.

The sergeant appraised the two men a moment longer, noticing their dress. They didn't look like trappers or traders with their expensive store-bought boots, dark striped pants, leather vests and heavy jackets, plus six-guns on their hips. He didn't mouth his thoughts, deciding instead it just might be first impressions.

'I'll try to talk to Crows, for you. If you mean to be around for a while it's best I know your names. We keep a journal in the office about anyone who happens to pass through here and where they're going.' He looked at both men expectantly.

'Ah, I'm Frank Jury, and my partner here is Delbert Hoyt.'

'All right then. I might be able to find a bunk for you two if you'd like to sleep inside, here?'

'No, I think we'll camp by our wagon after we take it back out. We want to be close to our goods. If we can meet those Crows tomorrow, we can get right down to business.'

'I'll see what I can do. I'd also offer you can eat with us tonight. We've got a pretty fair cook. You know the cavalry can't ride or fight on an empty stomach.'

'We might take you up on dinner. Hoyt here isn't much of a cook. Neither am I.'

THREE

In the cool shade of tall pines, the next morning Jury
and Hoyt sat on the tailgate of their wagon rolling ciga-
rettes. Looking up, Sergeant Cleary came into view
followed by two Crow Indians. Their long black hair
hung down both shoulders in tight braids, a white-
tipped eagle feather tucked in back. Both were naked
down to their waist and wearing deer-skin pants, a skin
breechcloth in front, with their feet covered in heavy
and ankle-high moccasins. Each carried an Enfield
Patterson rifle in .57 calibre, something of which Jury
took quick notice. The new Henry repeating rifles he
and Hoyt had hidden nearby were vastly superior to
those old muskets. The trio came to a stop, Cleary intro-
ducing the Crows.

'This is Red Moccasin and Blue Swallow. I told them
you two were traders who had come far to make medicine. If you talk slow and choose your words carefully,
you should be able to communicate with them. It does
take a bit of getting used to at first, until you get the
hang of it.'

Frank Jury stood away from the wagon, eyeing both Indians before extending his hand. The warriors only stared back stoically.

'They don't understand handshakes,' Cleary explained quickly. 'If you have some tobacco, offer them that. It's the way they trade out here before anything else.'

Jury reached into his jacket pocket, pulling out a pouch of Blackwell Tobacco, and Zig Zag cigarette papers in a flat cardboard holder. 'Do they know how to roll these?' he asked the sergeant.

'Not with your paper. Go ahead and show them anyway. When you do, offer them the finished smoke.'

Both men rolled a cigarette, folding the thin white paper over at the scam and licking them closed, before handing them to the Crows. The pair stared back at Cleary, then the wagon men, as the sergeant motioned for them to put the smokes in their mouth. Doing so with great reserve, Hoyt struck a match, lighting both.

'You have a blanket in your wagon?' Cleary asked.

'Yeah, we do,' Jury nodded.

'Spread it out on the ground, so we can sit and make some talk. That's how they like to trade, if they really have anything to trade at all. Like I told you earlier, they don't have much any white man could possibly want.'

'They might. We can trade for information,' Jury spoke up. 'Maybe we can learn some good trapping areas to work. We don't know the country up here like they do, and we don't want to run into any hostiles, either.' He was quick to make up his excuse.

'I guess that might do,' the sergeant nodded. Hoyt

retrieved a blanket from the wagon. Spreading it, all five men sat down, the Crows still not uttering a single word. 'If you have some goods to show them, why not bring them out now so they can see what they are?'

Both men brought out rolls of cloth, several containers of brightly coloured beads and cooking pots. Red Moccasin and Blue Swallow only glanced quickly at each other, picking up several items before laying them back down. Obviously, neither were impressed. Hoyt got up, digging around under the wagon canvas again. Coming back, he laid three axes, four leather-sheathed Bowie knives and half a dozen steel traps on the blanket. Red Moccasin was quick to pick up a Bowie knife, slowly turning it in his hands so the wide blade flashed in sunlight, matching the sudden gleam of interest in his eyes. For the first time he spoke.

'Cloth . . . and beads are for . . . women. This is for . . . warriors.' He held the knife higher, still admiring it.

The sergeant glanced at Jury, nodding ever so slightly at their first success.

'These axes are good, too.' Hoyt picked one up, handing it to Blue Swallow. 'You can chop wood with this.' He flashed a toothy grin for emphasis.

'Women . . . . chop wood. Warriors . . . no do,' Blue Swallow glared back.

'Sergeant Cleary.' A young orderly came running up at a trot. 'Captain wants to see you in his office right away, sir.'

'What for?' Cleary got to his feet, irritated at being interrupted.

'I don't know, sergeant. He only ordered me to find

you and bring you back.'

Cleary cussed quietly under his breath, looking down at the wagon men. 'Can you two keep this going without me until I get back?'

'Sure, we can,' Jury answered. 'We're just now getting the hang of it. You go ahead and see what your captain wants. We'll be right here when you get back. Take your time. We ain't going no place.'

'All right. I'll make this as quick as possible. Just remember to keep it simple so they understand everything.'

'We sure will,' Jury smiled, as Cleary started for the fort at a fast walk, orderly in tow. The moment he was out of earshot, Jury turned to Hoyt with a quick order. 'Get me one of them Henrys, and make it fast!'

The Crows looked at each other, wondering why the white man jumped to his feet and ran back behind the wagon out of sight. The moment Hoyt reappeared, they had their answer as Jury began talking low and fast.

'Listen to me, you two. You know where the Shoshone Indians live, don't you?'

Neither brave answered, staring at the shiny, new rifle as Hoyt sat down placing the long gun on the blanket, pushing it temptingly toward them.

'The Shoshone Indians,' Jury pressed again. 'I want you two to go find them and ask about an old white man who lives in their country and digs for gold, you savvy? You find out where he is, and I'll give you more rifles and cartridges, too. But you can't tell anyone else about it. No soldier boys, no one. Not even Cleary. It has to stay a secret between you two and us. You understand what I'm saying?'

Red Moccasin picked up the Henry, looking it up and down, testing its deadly weight, admiring the long barrel and cartridge tube underneath. For the first time since they'd sat down, the stoic look on both Crows' faces changed to one of real want. Red Moccasin turned to his blood brother, saying something neither white man could understand, before looking over his shoulder to be sure Cleary was out of sight.

'We . . . savvy.' He answered. 'No tell . . . soldiers. We go to . . . Shoshone village.'

'When?' Jury's voice crackled with excitement. 'How quick can you do it?'

'We go . . . in dark. No moon . . . tonight,' Blue Swallow answered, taking the rifle in his hands, admiring it with hungry eyes.

'How long before you get back here?' Hoyt questioned.

The Crows looked at each other, exchanging a few brief words. 'This many.' Red Moccasin held up eight fingers.

'All right, then. You two get to it. Me and Hoyt will stay right here until you get back with what I want to know. When you do, the rifles are yours. We'll pack up and leave the same day. I don't want to be around here with anyone else asking a lot of questions. Just remember you don't know anything about no rifles, even after we're long gone.'

The Crows got to their feet, starting away without looking back. Jury slapped Hoyt on the shoulder. A broad grin broke out on his face. 'We're gonna' get this done and pick up that extra hundred dollars, Sturgis promised us. You watch and see.'

'All I can say is, this better happen like we think or we'll both end up behind bars here or someplace else. Giving guns to Indians can get us hung. Even Sturgis's money can't buy us out of that!'

That night, under the first scattering of stars, Red Moccasin and Blue Swallow left their tepees, silently making their way to the Crows' big *ramuda* of horses grazing quietly in a pasture behind their village. Each man only carried a small pouch of dried food plus their rifles and extra cartridges. Both also carried the fear the Shoshones might kill them on sight before they could even ask about the strange white man living somewhere far back in the Tobacco Root Mountains, hammering away at his golden find. Red Moccasin had already thought about a way to save them if Standing Bear ordered their death. He told Blue Swallow he'd offer the Shoshone chief half the rifles to let them go if they could make the deal. He knew the Shoshones would want those rifles just as badly as he and his people did. Both warriors guided their horses higher through black timber into midnight mountains knowing how dangerous their journey was. Neither spoke a single word, each man with his own thoughts and fears. Their very lives were on the line.

Jesper Tubbs had no such worries. He had continued steadily chipping away at his golden quartz vein since his return from Eagle Buttes and the close call involving the men who tried to follow him. The first few days back, he worried about whether or not someone might still be trying to track him. Each morning he'd spend the first half hour perched on a rocky high point, squinting through an old pair of cavalry binoculars he'd traded from a drunken trooper years earlier. Although his eyesight wasn't that sharp any more, he still used the big glasses, scratched and filmy as they were, because they brought distant canyons up close and the thread of game trails he'd used coming back. Satisfied he was alone, he went back to work slowly building the pile of crushed, white quartz that had fascinated Standing Bear. His fortune grew ounce by ounce with it.

The two Crow horsemen closed in on the Shoshone village in the late afternoon of the fourth day of their long ride, which had seen them climbing higher as they went. Shoshone scouts intercepted them before the pair actually reached the big meadow dotted with dozens of tall teepees and horses grazing out back next to a small creek. They were quickly stripped of their weapons and their hands were tied behind their backs before they were led into the village, where a crowd quickly gathered around them. Small boys poked them with sharp, stick weapons. Others threw rocks, young men shouting threats, as they were being marched to Standing Bear's buffalo hide teepee. Being pulled to a stop, the braves escorting them called out for the chief to see the surprise they'd brought him. The teepee flap cover was pulled aside and Standing Bear stepped out, staring at the Crows. He slowly looked them up and down before stepping even closer. Red Moccasin and Blue Swallow stiffened at his approach. One whispered word, one small gesture of his hand, could mean a stone axe instantly smashing into the back of their heads, until Standing Bear spoke.

'Crows are . . . fools to ride into Shoshone land.' He uttered the words with pure disgust. 'You live next to white soldiers, and eat his food. Your people have become . . . sheep. You no longer know how to fight and die. Did you come here to die?'

Red Moccasin took in a deep breath. He had to talk fast, or die on the spot. He did not blink as he answered. 'Are the Shoshone so afraid of only two Crows that they tie our hands and take our horses and weapons? We did not come to fight, but to talk.'

'Talk . . . of what? What fool would send you here?' The chief questioned.

'We come to talk trade.' Blue Swallow found the courage to speak up.

'What could the Crows have that I would want? Do you trade for your lives? That is all you have,' Standing Bear challenged.

'Listen to me, Standing Bear,' Red Moccasin was quick to answer. 'The white man has new rifles that can be loaded once and shoot all day. We have seen these rifles. Two wagon men will trade them for information you hold.'

The chief's expression changed ever so slightly. Red Moccasin could see his interest rising. 'Show me these rifles and I won't let my braves kill you where you stand.'

'We do not have them yet. But we will if you give us the information we need, for these wagon men.'

'What information?'

'There is an old white man who lives in your mountains. Tell us where he is and the rifles will be ours. We'll give you half of them and cartridges, too.'

Standing Bear was stunned and confused how this simple information could produce the kind of rifles he wanted. Why would anyone want to know where a half crazy old white man's camp was, and give up so great a prize for it. It made no sense to him. There had to be more to it.

'Do the horse soldiers want to know this?' he finally asked.

'No,' Blue Swallow quickly assured him. 'These two white men came to the soldiers' fort with a wagon. They are the only ones who want to know. They did not tell us why.'

'With these rifles we can be powerful again,' Red Moccasin spoke up. 'Maybe we can even drive the white men and soldiers out of our land. Both your people and mine can live free again. You have that chance now to do it.'

The chief stepped back, still eyeing the pair suspiciously, but the thought of that power intrigued him greatly. He said something under his breath to his braves, who untied the Crows' hands. Blue Swallow massaged his wrists, trying to get circulation back, as Standing Bear spoke again.

'I will think on it tonight. You will stay here without your weapons. When the sun rises tomorrow, I will give you my answer.'

All that night a pair of Shoshone guards stood watch over the teepee into which the Crows were led. Neither brave slept, fearful that come dawn they could both be killed. When the first rays of sunlight lit the teepee walls, the two braves were led out in front of Standing Bear's teepee. He stepped out wrapped in a blanket, staring at the pair. For several tension-packed seconds he did not speak. When he did, both Crows swallowed in relief.

'Blue Swallow stays here until you bring back the rifles. You do not come back, he will die a slow death. Your name will always be remembered as a coward by your own people.'

Red Moccasin took in a deep breath. 'I still have to tell the wagon men where this white man lives, to get the rifles.'

The chief took his walking staff, drawing a crude picture in soft ground. He made a circle showing where the village was, then drew a straight line back over several small 'M' shapes, depicting mountain ranges, due west before bringing his staff down with a thud.

'This white man you seek lives two days' ride from here. He lives on white mountain. Now you ride fast for wagon men. I will not wait long for your return, and my rifles.'

Red Moccasin's horse was brought up. He was handed his rifle, knife and food pouch. Leaping atop his horse, he glanced down at Blue Swallow. 'I will come back, my brother,' he promised, digging his heels into the horse's flanks, starting away at a thundering gallop until he disappeared out of sight in thick timber at the far end of the big meadow. Blue Swallow watched him go, knowing his very life depended on his return. The Shoshone guards motioned him back toward the teepee. Passing Standing Bear, the chief said not one word. The look on his face said enough. Entering the teepee, Stone Horse uttered a short command to his braves. They took up positions outside to ensure their captive made no attempt to escape if all this Crow talk proved to be nothing but lies.

Red Moccasin drove his horse relentlessly down out of the mountains at a killing pace that left both horse and rider near collapse. He stopped only to water the animal and drink quickly himself. The savage pace paid off when he reached his village outside the fort three days later at night. Still driven by urgency, he went straight to the wagon men's camp. A slow twist of smoke curled up from the mound of ashes that was an evening fire. Both Jury and Hoyt lay under heavy canvas in the back of the wagon, sound asleep. The Crow came up, peering over the sideboards. Reaching down, he shook Jury to wake up. The reaction was instant and deadly. Struggling to sudden consciousness, Jury kicked off the canvas, coming up with his six-gun in his hand, fumbling to cock the hammer back for a shot at the dark shadow looming over him.

'No, white man . . . it is me . . . Red Moccasin!' The brave shouted in Jury's face, grabbing his gun hand and twisting the pistol away, as Hoyt woke up thrashing around wondering what all the commotion was about, trying to reach for his pistol, too.

Jury finally realized who it was. Sitting up, he rubbed sleepiness out of his eyes, rolling up on his knees. 'It's OK Hoyt. It's Red Moccasin. Get up and get a good fire going. I want to hear what he's got to say.'

New flames leapt to life in the fire pit, all three men standing around their growing crackle, as Jury spoke up. 'Well, did you find the Shoshones or not?'

'I find them. They hold my blood brother until . . . I ride back with rifles.'

'What about Tubbs? That's what I want to know. Did they tell you where he is or not? Get to it!'

'Standing Bear show me . . . I have map in head. When light comes I draw it for you on ground.'

'No, I ain't waiting that long. Hoyt, get me some paper and a pencil. I want this right now. And show me where the sun rises too, so I know what direction it is from Eagle Buttes.'

Red Moccasin carefully sketched out the map. Finishing, he handed it to Jury.

He took it, turning toward the fire to get a good, close look. 'You sure this is exactly what Standing Bear showed you?'

'Yes . . . me sure. Now you get rifles.'

Jury folded up the precious piece of paper, putting it inside his jacket, before turning to his partner, who had just buttoned up his coat. 'Go get the rifles and ammo boxes. Give them to him, then we'll hook up the horses and get out of here. I want to be long gone before dawn, and any of these soldier boys ever wake up!'

FOUR

Jesper Tubbs and Jenny had just reached their camp with another load of golden quartz as the sun reached its midday zenith. Jesper quickly caught the flash of colour of many horses coming down through the timber. It could only be the Shoshones again. The big white horse in the lead meant Standing Bear was back. Jesper was puzzled by that. The chief had visited only two weeks' earlier, why would he be back so soon? He tied Jenny off, standing with his hands on his hips, as the Shoshones reined to a stop in front of him. The first thing he noticed was the shiny, new rifles all were carrying.

'Howdy, Standing Bear.' Tubbs pulled at the brim of his worn-out hat. 'Sorta surprised to see you back here, but you know I'm always glad to have you.'

Jesper well knew the Indians' ways. They never came to the point of any meeting right off. Instead, they made small talk of other subjects before finally addressing their real reasons. This time Standing Bear surprised him. He made a quick motion for one of his

48

braves to begin filling a large skin bag he'd brought from the pile of shiny white quartz chips, before turning to Tubbs without getting off his horse.

'White men . . . look for you here,' he spoke.

'White men? What white men are you talking about? Were they soldier boys?'

'No. White men from town, far away.'

'You mean Eagle Buttes?'

'Maybe same.'

Jesper shuffled uneasily. 'Did you tell them where I am?'

The chief didn't answer for several long seconds, his eyes locked on the old man he still thought was half crazy. When he did, Tubbs breathed a big sigh of relief.

'I tell them . . . you over there,' he turned, pointing to another range of mountains far across the canyon.

A smile parted Jesper's fuzzy, whiskered face. He had to chuckle under his breath. Just as quickly, he knew how the Shoshones had gotten their hands on all those new rifles. Worry quickly followed. Who would want to know where he was so badly they'd take a chance trading rifles to Indians? That could end you up in prison, or worse.

'Did they say why they wanted to know?' He had to ask.

The chief only shook his head no, adding his own thoughts. 'We no want any white men here.'

'I feel the same way about it, Standing Bear. They'd only come to make trouble for your people and me. Thank you for keeping our little secret. Maybe I'll have to start keeping my eyes open from now on. If they ever did find me, they'd take all your quartz away, too. I know you don't want that to happen either.'

The brave finished filling the sack, remounting his horse. Standing Bear gave Tubbs one more long look before pulling his horse around and the Shoshones started back up the timber ridge, leaving the old man standing there thinking over this troubling turn of events. He wondered if they could be connected to the same men who tried to trail him when he left town weeks earlier after taking in his first load of ore. Wild talk back there of his gold strike could drive some men to take any risk, regardless of how dangerous, to learn his secret location. That could easily include murder too, when the maddening glitter of gold was in question. At least Jesper did know one thing for sure; he was now a hunted man, but not by any law. Far worse, he was being hunted by men to whom the law meant nothing. That made them the most desperate deadly men of all.

Frank Jury whipped the two-horse team ahead hard and fast with Delbert Hoyt hanging on for all he was worth. The clattering wagon bounced off rocks and skidded around sharp corners, but Jury wouldn't let up. His reckless pace paid off when the pair came wheeling down into town seven days later. Pulling to a stop in front of Sturgis's office, Hoyt looked over at his partner.

'You damned near killed us getting here. You know that, don't you?'

'Yeah, maybe I did, but look how much time I made up. Let's get inside and tell Sturgis we're ready for that hundred dollar bonus he promised us. We earned every cent of it for sure, sticking our necks out like we did.'

'We ain't gonna' have to wait long for that. He's already coming out.' Hoyt nodded toward the front door, as Sturgis stepped outside.

'You two get yourself in here, and you better have some good news for me or else!' Sturgis threatened, waving the pair up the stairs.

Hustled into his office, R.T. immediately began a barrage of questions about what the men had learned and who they'd seen and talked to. Jury began carefully explaining their meeting with Red Moccasin and Blue Swallow, plus the Crows' ride into Shoshone country to make the rifle trade. He embellished the danger and hardships of the trip plus having to deal with the Crows right under the nose of the military at the fort, to be sure Sturgis would come across with the promised bonus money. When R.T. grew impatient pressing for more details of where Tubbs' golden vein was hidden, Jury dramatically reached inside his jacket with a smug smile, producing the paper map.

'Hoyt and I brought you back this,' he announced, Sturgis instantly grabbed it out of his hands, unfolding it and spreading it on his desk. All three gathered around while R.T.'s hungry eyes devoured the simple, pencil drawing.

'It looks sort of rough, to me,' Sturgis scowled. 'How can we tell how far it is from here or in what direction?'

Hoyt pointed a finger at the dark circle that marked Fort Pakston, and the arrow at the top corner showing where the sun rose. 'That's east. Me and Frank figure it's about a ten-day ride from here to where the Crows say Tubbs is holed up. And they also said he lived on what they call a 'white mountain'. That probably means it has snow on it all year round. If you draw a line from here to that point, that's how we came up with the time to get there. It ain't gonna' be easy, but now we at least got a map to go by. We stuck our necks out pretty far to bring this back. That bonus money you promised us is the reason why.'

Sturgis ignored the plea, his eyes still going over the map as his quick mind worked devising a plan to take advantage of it. When he looked up at the pair again, he already had the details worked out. 'I'm going to hire six good riders who know the back country and how to use a six-gun. They'll have to be men who can stay in the saddle 'long as we have to, and I want all of them to have rifles and plenty of cartridges. You two are going along, too. That will make eight riders. I'll be nine.'

'You mean to go?' Jury questioned, the sudden rise in his voice obvious.

'This is too important for me not to. I don't want anyone else fouling up my orders. Besides, I'll have to have landmarks, so I can record a deed claim once we find the location of Tubbs' gold.'

'What about Wickman?' Hoyt wondered.

'He stays here in town. He can keep his eye on things while we're gone. Besides, he could only trail Tubbs two miles last time he tried. I don't need him for this.'

'Ahh . . . what about the bonus money you promised us?' Hoyt boldly tried a second time, hoping Sturgis wouldn't explode after being asked again.

'You two did all right. Now I'll do better once we ride out there and find that old coot's hideout.'

R.T. crossed the room to a large, black wheel safe in one corner of the office. Keeping his back to the pair, he worked the dial combination back and forth several times until he pulled the heavy steel door open. Retrieving a flat, wide metal box, he came to the desk and opened it. Inside, in neatly stacked and wrapped bundles, lines of one hundred dollar bills filled the box to the top. Pulling out two bills, he handed them to Jury and Hoyt.

'You keep doing me good, there's more where this came from.' He closed the lid and returned the container to the safe, while talking over his shoulder. 'After we get rid of Tubbs and I file my claim, I might give both of you a little raise, if everything works out like I expect it to.'

The pair glanced at each other, both thinking exactly the same thing; if something tragic happened to their boss on their long journey into the Tobacco Root Mountains, that safe could be blown and the money in it was enough to support both of them after they made their way across the border into Mexico on fast horses. There was enough there to ensure neither one of them would ever have to break sweat again in their entire lives.

Sturgis came back to the desk, standing with both hands resting on it as he eyed the two men. 'Tomorrow, I start putting together what we'll need to make this trip. I want you two to talk to any pals you know who can

be part of it. Remember, they need to be able to ride
hard and shoot straight. I have a couple in mind myself,
but you might come up with a few that are worthwhile.
I don't want any bar flies or street loafers. I need men
who can take orders and carry them out. Soon as I get
all the equipment together, we'll mount up and leave
town. I'm about to get me the richest gold mine in all
the Rocky Mountains, and by God, no one or nothing
is going to stop me from doing it!'

The frantic pace R.T. Sturgis set for himself was
impressive. Food lists, camp gear, tarps, blankets, extra
cartridges, tools, ropes and pack mules were all
checked off his list one by one, day after day, with no
thought to expense. Merchants in Eagle Buttes were
eager to help selling him all he needed. The town actually had a modest sale boom because of his buying
spree. By the end of the first week he'd picked the men
he wanted, and was closing in fast on the task he'd set
for himself. The following Wednesday his small army of
men and equipment was mounted up ready to ride,
everyone gathering in the saddle in front of his office.
R.T. stepped outside, surveying the riders, pack mules
and bystanders lining the street watching. This was the
biggest event of his life. He almost smiled in satisfaction, he was so pleased. Years of lying, cheating, forging
false documents and paying men to kill anyone who got
in his way was now paying off in his biggest grab of
greed ever. He could not let it pass without an
announcement for all to see, hear and record.

'Men, I'm paying each of you good money to follow
my orders each and every day we're on the trail. I

expect all of you to carry them out without complaint. We'll likely be gone several weeks, I'm not sure yet exactly how long. If anyone quits on me, they won't be paid, period. You stick it out until the end, you'll all make good money. If anyone has any questions, ask them now. Once we ride out of here, I don't want to hear it.'

One man in front slowly raised his hand. Sturgis nodded at him. 'It sounds to me like we're heading into Shoshone country. If that's so, I hear they can be big trouble.'

'From what I know about it, they might be. But I'm also told they move around a lot. We might never see any of them. Besides, we've got enough firepower to handle anything that might come our way. I'm not worried about it, neither should you. Anyone else?'

Another rider spoke up. 'You expect us to use all these tools you've got loaded on the mules? I didn't hire on to do day labour.'

'The tools are only to dig ore samples. I'm not going to start any full-scale mining, at least not yet. Anyone else got something they want to get off their chest?' The riders sat silent this time. 'All right then, let's get to it!'

The boardwalks leading out of town were packed with excited men, women and children, eager to watch the caravan depart. The town's one-room school house had even been closed for the big event. With R.T. Sturgis in the lead, a long line of riders and pack mules started down the street. Sturgis was flanked by Jury and Hoyt. Just to be certain his big send-off had an unforgettable flair, Sturgis had paid a small band of musicians hastily thrown together from local saloons to play 'Camptown Races'. Drums thundered, cymbals crashed and bugles blared as R.T. rode past, tipping his hat to the crowd, who responded by shouting and applauding at the spectacle he'd created. Excited talk rippled through everyone that this great benefactor to Eagle Buttes would very likely be a shoo-in to be elected state senator, or even possibly governor if and when the territory actually became a state. It was a grand exit the like of which the citizens of Eagle Buttes had never seen before and would never forget. It was also one R.T. Sturgis would never see repeated either.

Once out of town, the caravan of riders started up the first steep climb into timber, Jury and Hoyt taking the lead and showing the way they'd tried to follow Jesper Tubbs all those weeks earlier, losing his tracks. But Sturgis had another ace up his sleeve for that problem. He'd hired a strange man named Zack Hitch, who had a reputation for being able to track any man, over any ground, as sure as an Indian. Hitch lived alone outside town in a small cabin. He fed himself on wild game killed using traps or snares he'd set to save precious cartridges. He was a physically small man; wiry, wild-eyed and made even more loathsome by a deeply scared, misshapen face. Both eyes seemed to be tilted in a different direction. His fearsome look was the result of an attack by a grizzly bear that he'd caught in one of his traps but which broke lose when he closed in to kill it. The enraged beast came over the top of him, mauling him savagely with razor-sharp claws and teeth. He got off one lucky shot straight up into the animal's heart, killing the brute. Dragging himself back to his cabin, he laid there for days, too weak to move from loss of blood, before somehow climbing on his horse and making it into town for help. Children who saw him on his rare trips into Eagle Buttes recoiled in horror, running screaming to their parents. However, the disfigured hermit was exactly what he'd said he was; a first-rate tracker of both man and animals, from years living in the wilds.

Jury and Hoyt reined to a stop, pointing ahead as Hitch and R.T. rode up. 'This is the last spot we got any look at Tubbs. He was above us, up there, just going out of sight.' Jury nodded, up the steep climb.

Hitch eased his horse forward. Leaning over in the saddle, he studied the ground with his one good eye, before straightening up squinting into brush and jack pines ahead. Without uttering a single word, he wagged his finger for them to follow him higher, the long line of riders moving again. Reaching a little level bench, Hitch got down, kneeling to brush away tufts of dead grass and leaves, revealing Jenny's old hoof print. He straightened up, looking higher. Turning to Sturgis, he spoke for the first time.

'I got 'em,' he nodded. Mounting up again and taking the lead, he urged his horse higher into tall timber.

R.T. turned to Jury and Hoyt with a sly grin on his face. 'I got me the right man to puzzle out Tubbs' trail, didn't I? He's as good as dead right now, no matter how far away he is!'

For the next five days, Jack Hitch carefully followed

the faint tracks, leading his fellow riders up one mountain side and down the other. At various times he lost the track and had to backtrack to pick it up again. Over rocky ground he got down, moving slowly and leading his horse while looking for an upturned rock, or telltale scrape of hoofs over hard stone. Back in timber and brush again, he found broken twigs and branches. If he was lucky, several times he found a dried up pile of Jenny's mule biscuits. Each evening when they made camp, Sturgis questioned him endlessly on how close he thought they were to finding Tubbs' secret location, and how much longer it would take. Hitch only shrugged he didn't know for sure, but did say the tracks were getting easier to read and that might be an indication they were closing in. It drove Sturgis crazy that he couldn't get an exact answer, but Hitch did tell him this much.

'Whoever this man of yours is, he's about half mule himself. He don't stop for nothing, and don't leave much to follow when he does, but I'm still on 'em. If we don't get a storm to wash out his tracks, I'll take you right to him. That's one thing you can count on for sure.'

Sturgis bit at his tin coffee cup in exasperation. Not only was day after day in the saddle beginning to wear on him, but he'd developed a fearsome case of being saddle sore. It had become so bad he walked with a slow limp, feeling like he was sawed in half right through the middle of the expensive, new riding pants he'd bought for the trip. What none of the men were aware of, not even Zack Hitch, was that they were not travelling into the Tobacco Root Mountains alone. A small band of Shoshone scouts out hunting had seen them far across the canyon two days earlier and had begun shadowing the tiny dots that were the line of riders. Count Coups, the Shoshone group's leader, decided to send a fast rider to Standing Bear, warning him about the white invaders, and that they seemed to be moving closer in the direction of the Shoshone village, possibly to attack it. He chose the youngest brave, Spotted Pony, to make the ride and sound the alarm.

'Ride fast and do not stop until you reach our village,' he ordered the eager young man. 'Tell Standing Bear we will not attack these white man until he brings more warriors here. You will show him the way. Go now, young one.'

Spotted Pony led his horse, on foot at a trot, out of sight back into thick pines, until he was sure his departure could not be seen from across the canyon. Mounting up, he started away at a breakneck pace, ducking low to avoid pine spears and streaking through timber like a fleeting shadow. The teenage warrior rode as fast as the winter wind for the next four days until he arrived at the village early on the morning of the fifth. A throng of men, women and children instantly gathered around him after he pulled his exhausted pony to a stop in front of Standing Bear's teepee. Hearing the commotion outside, the chief pulled the flap aside, stepping out as the young Shoshone blurted out his message of danger.

'Count Coups has sent me ... we have seen many white riders coming toward the village. He says he will not attack until you arrive with more braves. I will show you the way back.'

Standing Bear's eyes narrowed and his face broke in alarm. With a short order and wave of his hand, braves ran for their teepees to get rifles and pistols and prepared to ride. The chief asked Spotted Pony if he was still strong enough to return. His quick nod was all the answer he needed. While the chief gathered his own weapons inside his teepee, he told his woman, Dark Eyes, that if he did not return in victory, she was to abandon the village and move everyone even farther back into the mountains. Then his thoughts quickly turned to the puzzle why white men had so suddenly decided to come deep into Shoshone country. Were they white soldiers? Spotted Pony had made no mention of them being that. Could it have something to do with the pair of Crow warriors, and his trade for information of where Jesper Tubbs might be. If that was the case and he was able to kill or drive the white men out, he might have to change his mind about the crazy old man who crushed rocks and seemed harmless. Maybe he wasn't so harmless at all.

FIVE

The big evening campfire crackled and popped as the flames danced higher while R.T. and his men sat in a circle eating a dinner meal of beans, salt pork and pilot bread crackers all washed down with hot black coffee. Sturgis, Jury and Hoyt sat together discussing the day's progress and what might lay ahead. Sturgis did most of the talking while Hitch thoughtfully chewed on a piece of hardtack, largely ignoring them. Instead, his eyes wandered out beyond camp into the pitch black surrounding them, his ears cocked listening to every night sound. Somewhere out there the high trill of a quail calling instantly got his attention. He stopped eating. Lowering his coffee cup, he strained to hear it again. There is was, from somewhere across the canyon. Reaching over, he pulled at R.T.'s jacket to get his attention.

'What is it, Hitch?' Sturgis turned toward his tracker.

'We got company ... and it ain't no white men either.'

'What are you talking about? We haven't seen

another living soul since we left town.'

'I'm not talking about white folks.' Hitch slowly shook his head, staring hard at Sturgis with his one good eye.

'Who else then?'

'Indians.'

'What Indians? We haven't seen any sign of them or anyone else. Why bring up something like that now? It'll only make everyone nervous. We don't need any of that.'

'I bring it up because quail don't call at night, that's why.'

Jury stopped eating. He studied the tracker's face, made even more grotesque by flickering shadows of firelight, before speaking. 'Hey, he's right about that. Quail only call in the daytime.'

Hoyt looked at his pal, Hitch and back to R.T. 'That sounds right to me, too.' His voice suddenly had a nervous tinge to it.

Sturgis stood up, followed by Jury and Hoyt. Turning in a slow circle, all three peered out into the inky blackness surrounding them. The night was dead still again.

'You sure you know what you're talking about?' R.T. turned back to Hitch. 'I don't hear anything.'

Zack didn't answer right away, staring back at Sturgis. Trying to explain and warn someone who thought they knew everything, even something this dangerous, was like talking to a child. He decided to give it just one more try. 'They're out there someplace watching us. Probably have been for days staying out of sight. Some young buck made a mistake and used the wrong night call. We won't hear it again. From here on out we better be ready for anything.'

'You mean a gunfight?' R.T. questioned. 'Who would be crazy enough to take us on with all the firepower we have with these men here in camp? No one is that dumb!'

'Who?' Zack mocked him. 'Twice as many Shoshones, that's who.'

'You're letting the boogeyman get into your head over nothing. Drop the subject before you get everyone else all riled up over nothing. Tomorrow is going to be just like every other day since we left. We'll keep on riding into these mountains getting closer to finding Tubbs while we do so. I don't want to hear any more of this "bird calling" in the night baloney. Keep it to yourself. That's an order!'

In the blackness across the canyon Standing Bear's eyes focused on the distant campfire, carefully counting the number of men sitting around it. He did it a second time to be certain the number was correct, before leaning closer and whispering to Count Coups.

'Tomorrow on the cliff trail, we will take them when they are halfway up, riding in line.'

'They will die like rabbits in a snare.' Count Coups' smile was lost to the dark. 'These white men are too foolish to live any longer than that.'

'We must kill all of them. No one can escape to tell others or the horse soldiers. We cannot let them come into our land, too.' The chief nodded. The pair silently got to their feet, disappearing back into timber up the canyon where the rest of their braves waited.

At the first hint of dawn, Zack Hitch was already up, feeding last night's smoky ashes new wood. While the rest of the men slept, he walked to the edge of the clearing, eyes searching dark timber across the canyon for any sign of movement. He saw none, but his sixth sense still told him he was right about the previous evening's warnings. The Shoshone were still out there. He could feel it in the misty, morning air. Even the long hair on the back of his neck tingled with electricity. Big trouble was coming and R.T. Sturgis was hell-bent on riding everyone right into it. Hitch had seen early on that Sturgis was completely out of his element roughing it out here in wild back country. His big money and general attitude that no one knew anything else but him meant he was destined to end up with a Shoshone arrow or bullet in his back. Hitch made a little promise to himself when that became apparent. He would avoid at all costs ending up the same way.

One by one the crackling pop of the fire began waking up the rest of the men. Jury and Hoyt were first to sit up, throwing off their wool blankets. Delbert looked over at his pal, nodding toward Hitch.

'Don't he ever sleep?' he questioned in a low voice.

'I don't know. But if there's anyone staying awake at night in this bunch, I want it to be him. Especially after what he said last night.'

'Yeah, maybe so,' Hoyt grumbled, both men pulling on their boots and jackets before getting up and walking over to the delicious warmth of the fire.

Jury slid the big coffee pot up close to the flames. In five minutes it was bubbling hot. He poured himself a cup. Sipping at the black liquid, he walked over to Hitch, who still stood at the edge of camp, studying the terrain across the canyon.

'You still think there's trouble out there?' Jury asked.

'Yup, I know they are. You better tell that boss of yours to start believin' it too, or men are going to die because he's too damn stubborn for his own good, or anyone else's either.'

'No one can tell Sturgis much of anything. He sorta' thinks he know it all, or what he don't he can buy with all his money.'

'Death don't need any money, jus' someone dumb enough not to see it coming. I figure today or maybe tomorrow, we're going to see some of it. Him too.'

Jury didn't comment this time. Instead he walked back to Hoyt, warming his hands over the fire. 'What was that all about?' Delbert asked.

'Hitch says there's going to be trouble from the Indians. I know one thing for sure, I'll be riding with my rifle over my lap today, not in its scabbard. You better do the same. If he's right, we might have to fight our way out of here.'

By mid-morning the sun shone well above the arrow-shaped pine tops. The long line of riders came down a side hill with Hitch in the lead, reining his horse to a stop at the bottom. A shallow creek gurgled through the canyon. The elk trail they'd been travelling on crossed it and then started up the other side. Hitch's eye narrowed as he studied the steep climb. R.T. came riding up alongside him.

'Why are we stopping? We're making good time. Let's keep at it.'

Without turning to look at him, the tracker still eyed the way up. 'I don't like the look of this.' He poked his chin up the trail. 'Riders can only go up one at a time, like ducks in a row. It's a bad spot to get caught short in.'

'Are you going to start that again like last night? We can't go around this. That will take too much time. If you're too scared to try, I'll take the lead myself.'

'Better not. Better look this over for a bit before someone gets themselves killed.'

Sturgis, always a man of action, said something under his breath before twisting in the saddle and waving his men forward with a shout, kicking his own horse around Hitch and starting across the creek.

Zack Hitch reached down, pulling his rifle out of its scabbard. Holding it in one hand, he reined his horse around, letting Jury and Hoyt move in behind their boss. Slowly, one by one, the riders started up filling the trail nose to tail, labouring higher. Halfway to the top, R.T. turned back eyeing Hitch, a grim smile on his face. 'See what I said,' he yelled back. 'When you start worrying about that boogeyman of yours, you're fighting ghosts that don't exist. Maybe next time you'll remember what. . . .'

Sturgis never finished the sentence. He was cut short by a thunderous volley of sudden rifle fire coming from a line of low jack pines at the top of the trail, where Standing Bear and his warriors lay hidden watching the riders come up. Blue spears of rifle smoke spurted from the tree line as the new Henry rifles spat shot after shot of hot lead and death on hapless men jerked from their saddles. Screaming horses and men fell off the steep cliff face, many dead or dying before splashing into the creek below. R.T.'s horse collapsed from under him, throwing him head over heels and knocking him unconscious, tumbling like a rag doll into the icy water below. Suddenly submerged and unable to breath, the cold shocked him back to consciousness. He struggled up to his knees, spitting and coughing before trying to suck in a lungful of air. Geysers of bullet hits erupted close around him from the very same rifles he'd used to bribe the Crows.

At the top of the trail, the Shoshones ran from cover, continuing their murderous rain of rifle fire on the few remaining riders struggling to stay alive. Sturgis lunged for the bank, bumping between the bodies of dead men floating by face down, the wild look of fear and desperation on his bloody face. Where were Jury and Hoyt? They seemed to have vanished in all the shooting, shouting and bloodshed. Zack Hitch was nowhere in sight either. R.T. wiped the blood from his eyes. There was Hitch whipping his horse into timber disappearing up the trail they'd all come down on. Sturgis was frantic to find a horse. He came to his feet running, falling down, pulling himself up again. Suddenly out of the corner of his eye he saw Jury and Hoyt riding double, charging across the creek in a big fan of spray, more bullets erupting in the water around them.

'Frank . . . wait . . . don't leave me, come back . . .

FRANK!' he screamed at the top of his lungs.

The riders reached the far bank with Delbert hanging on behind Jury for all he was worth. In desperation, Sturgis pulled his pistol. Still running he fired a wild volley of shots at the pair. Hoyt suddenly stiffened to a bullet in his back, grabbing at Jury's jacket and trying desperately not to fall off. The horse spun and bucked as Hoyt fell to the ground allowing Sturgis to close in. R.T. clawed for the saddle, frantically trying to pull himself up. Jury's reaction was sudden and equally violent. He kicked his boss full in the face, driving him backwards onto the ground and nearly knocking him unconscious a second time. Sturgis rolled up onto his knees, head spinning and trying to regain his feet. The last thing he saw of Frank Jury was him digging his heels into the horse's flanks as rider and animal disappeared up the trail at a run into dark timber. Sturgis looked wildly around. Standing Bear and his braves were mounting horses and coming down over the top of the trail. He had to do something fast. With no other choice, he began running up the willow-lined creek until he couldn't run any more, collapsing in numbing cold water up to his waist in a thick copse of winter-piled brush and tree limbs. Shivering uncontrollably, he dared peeking back downstream where the Shoshones were dispatching the few wounded men still left alive with pistol shots and axes, stripping them of their weapons. By some bloody miracle, R.T. Sturgis was still alive. He dared not move a muscle until after dark when the slaughter ended and the victorious Indians had finally left him alone in the dark canyon with the smell of death hovering over it. Slowly, Sturgis began to access his situation.

Eagle Buttes lay at least a week's ride away over dozens of miles of mountains. He was bloody, broken, without food or horse, yet even now the white-hot fire of revenge was slowly burning in his shattered body. That desire for revenge could keep a man alive, regardless of how high the odds were stacked against him. He swore to himself he would not give up and die like all the others. Somehow, some way he'd find his way out of these deathly Tobacco Root Mountains to walk the streets of Eagle Buttes again. When he did he'd kill Frank Jury on sight. Not one living soul would blame him for it after he had told how Jury had abandoned him to die at the hands of the savage Shoshones. Painfully, step by step, Sturgis pulled himself up to his feet before heading off along the long trail into night-time timber.

Four days later, Jesper Tubbs led Jenny up toward his camp with another lode of precious quartz bulging in leather sacks over her back. Looking up, he was surprised to see mounted Indians already waiting for him. He wondered why Standing Bear had returned so soon after his last visit. The answer he was about to receive would astound and shock him like nothing else could. The chief's dark eyes followed the old man as he climbed those last few yards into his camp. As usual, Jesper cracked a whiskery smile and gave a quick wave of his hand.

'Well howdy again, Standing Bear. I'm surprised to

see you back here so soon, but you know I'm always glad when you and your braves ride in. I imagine you're here to get more of my shiny white stones you like so much, huh?'

The chief didn't answer for several long seconds. Jesper quickly saw there was something else on his mind. His stare and posture spelled trouble might be brewing, although he couldn't guess what. After the long silence, Standing Bear spoke.

'Many armed white men rode into my country. We had to . . . kill them. They come here to find . . . you!' He pointed an accusing finger at Tubbs.

'Me? No white man knows I live here. You know that to be true yourself.'

'No! Crows want to know this, but I tell them lie . . . to trade for rifles. These white men come here . . . Crows told them. If horse soldiers know this we will have to fight them, too. You will have to leave. Go back to white man's town . . . or more will come looking for you . . . and your white rocks.'

'But Standing Bear, I can't jus' pack up and leave. I live like the Shoshone, right here in these mountains. I have for years. If I go back to Eagle Buttes, bad men will kill me for sure, and they will come here. I thought we were blood brothers? I've slept in your teepee and ate at your campfires. I've lifted your babies and told you how beautiful they are. Have you forgotten all that?'

The chief's furrowed brow was a sign of sudden indecision. Maybe, he thought, anger and concern had clouded his mind. Everything Jesper had said was true. He was different from all the others. But was it enough to risk letting him stay after the killing battle in the canyon? Tubbs saw his moment of confusion, quickly following up before Standing Bear could make up his mind.

'This country has been yours and mine for many moons. If the white soldiers come here and force you and your people to take down your teepees and tell Dark Eyes her and your children must leave and live on a reservation far away, will you go?'

The stinging question brought an immediate response, just as Tubbs hoped. 'I would never go . . . I would fight them . . . always!'

'Yes, I know you would. And that's the same way I feel now. This is where my heart is, just like you and your people. What man wants to be told he must leave his home? We may have different-coloured skin, but we are both blood brothers to these mountains and our way of life. Please don't tell me I have to go. I would die, too, if you did.'

The tall Shoshone finally broke his gaze away from the old man. His eyes caressed the high mountains around them. White streaks of last winter's snow still shone bright blue in shadowed canyons. Big, fluffy clouds with grey bellies hung motionless over the peaks. Yes, this was his precious home and one he'd fight and die for. Maybe it would be his last stand against white men and their soldiers, but he would not give it up. After a long pause, he looked back on Tubbs.

'If white men come again . . . you must go. You can stay . . . now. I will talk with spirits for help.'

'Thank you my brother.' Jesper breathed a sigh of

relief. 'I know the spirits will tell you you've made a wise decision. No more white men will come. I am sure of it.'

The chief lingered only a moment longer before reining his horse around as braves got in line behind him. Tubbs stood and watched them ride up the steep ridge, but now his mind was equally troubled, too. Who were these men Standing Bear had spoken of? Surely, once the word got out there would be more battles that might even include the cavalry. Jesper's own future suddenly seemed in real jeopardy, too. After years of living and chasing a golden dream with nothing to show for it, he'd now found a fabulous vein of gold. Would he lose it all because of greedy men and circumstances over which he had no control? Even worse, had he put his old friend Standing Bear and all his people in real harm, too? It seemed so. Long after the Shoshone riders went out of sight, Tubbs still stood there wondering if it would all end in even more bloodshed.

Frank Jury fled the massacre, riding like a man possessed. Every night when he stopped worn out, his nerves frayed, and tried to get a few hours of sleep, he only pitched and turned until he sat up and prayed that dawn would come so he could ride again. He jumped at every sound, at every creak of wind that swayed the timber and at every ghostly image out there in the shadows. Once, when he fell into a short fitful sleep, he dreamed that R.T. Sturgis came stumbling toward him from out of the dark. He sat up with a cry, waving the six-gun clutched in his hand, until he realized it was all another nightmare. He gave up trying to sleep, spending the remainder of that night sitting with his back propped up against a tree, wondering if Sturgis was really dead or not. He had to be. He'd seen all the other men jerked from their horses, dead before they fell into the water or hit the ground. No way could R.T. survive a savage attack like that. At the first thin hint of dawn, he quickly saddled up and started out again, convinced that he was the only man left alive to tell the tale exactly as he pleased.

But Jury was not alone. Somewhere on the trail ahead of him, Zack Hitch had also survived the murderous ambush and was making his way back to civilization, too. He suffered no such problems as Jury. He'd tried to warn Sturgis of impending danger and been ignored. As far as he was concerned, Sturgis had gotten exactly what he deserved. He also felt little remorse for the rest of the men, none of whom he knew anyway. They knew the risks and took their chances for money. What did concern him was about his pay as head guide. As was Sturgis's usual business dealings, he'd only paid Hitch half of his promised three hundred dollars, the other half to be collected on the successful return of the trip. With Sturgis obviously dead, he was out one hundred fifty dollars of money he'd counted on and badly needed, especially after this disaster. The law would surely get involved in what had happened sooner or later. He wanted no part of it. Maybe, he concluded, it was best to simply get home, lay low, and avoid everyone as he'd always done.

Two days after Hitch arrived at his cabin, Frank Jury rode out of the thick pines and pulled to a stop.

Through the scattered branches he saw the first images of buildings below and the smoky haze hanging over Eagle Buttes. He'd made it back to the safety of civilization, finally leaving behind the demons that had haunted him each night. The emotion of the moment and his poor physical condition suddenly overwhelmed him. Tears ran down his dirty, whiskered face and his hands quivered holding the reins. It took a bit to force himself back under control. He'd beaten all the odds stacked against him and was still alive to lie to everyone how he'd done it. When he made up the rest of the story with more lies and his own bravado, he'd be the town hero. The first place he headed for was Cas Wickman's office, pouring out his version of what happened and how Sturgis was killed by the Shoshones.

Wickman sat dumbfounded, mouth open at Frank's sudden appearance and the wild story he poured out. He looked Jury up and down. His clothes were torn and dirty, his gaunt face scratched and cut. Cas shook his head getting to his feet, but already thinking that, with his boss dead, he was now in complete control of everyone and everything in town, including R.T.'s money and holdings.

'How'd you make it back here without getting killed yourself?' he asked as he eyed Jury while nervously running his hands through his thinning hair.

'I guess it was a miracle. I damn near didn't. I've got to get me something to eat and drink. I'm about half starved to death.'

'We've got another problem and it might even be bigger than what happened to you and Sturgis. All his personal money and business holdings have to be dealt with. He never let me in on any of that, but now I'll have to figure out what to do about it. He had no wife or kids I ever heard him talk about. What do you think about that?'

'Well . . . you're the sheriff aren't you? You take control of all of it and we'll work it out from there. We don't need any lawyers sticking their noses into anything, and I'll tell you something else now that all this has happened; me and Hoyt had planned to blow his safe, then take all the cash and clear out. There's enough denaro in there to last a lifetime. We both saw it. They're both dead and so is everyone else. It's just you and me. I say we do what we damn well please.'

Cas came back to his chair, sitting down and trying to put everything together. It was all too much, too fast. His hand pulled at his jaw. Glancing at Jury, he came up with the only answer he could think of right now.

'Ahhh . . . I need time to think on it, Frank. Let's not do something too quick we might regret later. It's a big thing to make any mistakes on, and could lead to a whole lot of trouble. I'm still sheriff. I've got control of it all. Let's just take it easy for a little while. That way we'll both stay in the clear.'

'You can think all you want, but don't take too long. I'm not going to hang around here and watch grass grow. We've got a fortune right in our hands. I'm not going to watch it slip away into anyone else's. You make up your mind pretty quick. This is the chance of a lifetime. I don't expect another one any time soon. I mean to take it with or without you!'

SIX

But R.T. Sturgis was not dead. Against all odds, he was driven on by the burning hate of revenge, day after day, staggering forward until his legs gave out and he dropped to the ground crawling. Hunger and thirst racked his body, but he kept going. He ate anything he could find, including roots and once a few dried up berries on a bush. He ate that leaves, stems and all. Further along, he found some kind of white fungus growing on the side of a fallen tree. He devoured it despite its evil taste, but that night he rolled on the ground moaning, legs pulled up to his stomach from the pain, thinking he would surely die before dawn. He did not. One thing that saved him was finding a mule deer killed by a mountain lion. He hungrily gnawed on scraps of dried meat still left on the ribs, until he had no more strength and lay on his back staring up until the stars came out and he gave a short prayer that the big cat did not return to kill him, too. At dawn he rolled over and began again pulling himself across the ground foot by foot, yard by yard.

For several days, Frank Jury basked in the glory of his often-told tale of survival from the murderous onslaught of the savage Shoshones. He had quickly become the talk of the town everywhere he went. Free drinks were on the house and even free meals at eateries. As a bona fide hero, he played the part to the hilt, but his patience with Wickman to make up his mind was wearing thin. Once all Jury had been thought of was a paid gun hand doing Sturgis's bidding. Now he became almost respected and admired. He walked the streets of Eagle Buttes with a certain swagger in his step never seen before. Yet even his good luck and the lies that spawned them could not last forever. Two weeks was the limit.

Two ten-year-old twin boys, Daniel and David Marks, were playing cowboys and Indians at the end of town by sneaking through timber and brush trying to ambush each other. Daniel played the dashing cavalry officer, his brother fancied himself as the daring and dangerous Indian chief, Cochise. Scurrying from one piece of cover to the other, they shot imaginary bullets from stick rifles in mock battle, until David ran around the trunk of a big pine, coming to a sudden stop. On the ground in front of him lay the twisted body of a man face down. His ragged clothes were dirty and torn, his matted hair stuck with weeds, dirt and grass. David yelled for his brother, who came at a run, both boys staring down wide-eyed at the pitiful figure.

'Is he . . . dead?' Daniel wondered almost whispering.

'I don't know, but we'd better run and tell Paw about

it real quick.'

Daniel pushed his stick rifle down, poking the prostrate form. A small moan of life came back and the body twitched slightly.

'Holy smokes, he's alive!' David shouted. 'Come on, let's get out of here!'

Frank Jury was leaning back in the barber's chair getting a shave when the noise of people shouting out on the street got his attention. 'What's all the ruckus about out there?' he asked the man in a striped shirt who was carefully trimming his beard with a pearl-handled straight edge razor.

'I don't know.' The barber turned away, looking outside. 'Sounds like they're yelling about someone getting a doctor. Oh, now I see it. They've got someone lying in that wagon going by.' Another shout brought the name. 'Hey, they say they've got R.T. Sturgis in there. I thought you said he was dead?'

Jury erupted out of the chair, white towel still wrapped around his neck, causing the barber to jump back wild-eyed to keep from cutting him. Rushing to the door, he looked up the street at the passing wagon.

'That can't be,' he shouted. 'He's got to be dead, like I said!'

Back inside he quickly fished two bits out of his pocket, tossing them atop the marbled counter, before whipping shaving cream off his face.

'Here,' he said. 'I'm done.'

'But you've only got half a shave?' the barber protested.

'I don't have time for any more right now.'

Jury exited the shop with the barber following him outside, watching his unfinished customer striding quickly up the street toward Cas Wickman's office.

'Huh. Odd duck.' The barber said under his breath. 'Never shaved half a man before. Wonder what his rush is?'

Jury burst through the door into the sheriff's office to find Wickman sitting at his desk eating lunch. 'I got some bad news for both of us!' He blurted out.

'Like what?' Cas looked up.

'It looks like Sturgis is still alive. They just brought him down the street in back of a wagon. Somehow he must have made it back here. Don't ask me how!'

Cas quickly came to his feet, rushing out the door and seeing the wagon surrounded by a growing crowd of people, heading for the doctor's office. His face turned grim at the realization.

'If that is R.T., you can forget about any idea of me helping you blow that safe, I'll tell you that right now. I don't want any part of it, not with the chance he just might recover. If you're smart, you'll forget it, too. If you went ahead with something like that he'd hire an army of men to run you down wherever you went. You couldn't run far enough, fast enough. You said you were certain he was dead. What happened to that?'

'Last time I saw him he was good as dead. The Indians were killing everyone, and he was afoot without a horse. I barely made it back myself. Maybe we can still get lucky and he might die, anyway? If he doesn't, he might need a little help, and this time I'd be sure he didn't survive.'

'Now wait a minute, Frank. I'm not going to be part of any murder, not for you or all that money either. That's asking too much.'

'You've got a short memory, Cas. Remember when we went after Tubbs that first time. You were ready to do whatever you had to then. That didn't bother you none. Now you want to crawfish out?'

'That was different, and you know it. We could have taken care of the old man and left him for the wolves, once R.T. was done with him. Killing Sturgis now, right here in town, is something else again. He might not be loved by anyone around here, but something like that can put a rope around your neck, and I mean for both of us. Count me out, Frank!'

Jury didn't answer this time. It was clear Wickman wouldn't go along with his plans to finish off their boss once and for all. That didn't mean he'd give up on the idea. There had to be at least a hundred thousand dollars sitting in that safe, and he meant to get his hands on it no matter what it took. He knew Doctor Caldwell's office at the far end of town sometimes hosted badly injured patients in an extra bedroom for several days where he could continue to work on them. Sturgis would likely end up there too, in the kind of shape he had to be in. He decided, without saying so to Wickman, that he'd pay Sturgis a visit. Night time would be the best time, but not by knocking on the door, either.

When Sturgis regained consciousness two days later, haltingly whispering the tale of the Shoshone ambush and murder of his men to Caldwell, the town went wild. People heard the news with talk of revenge, and questioned the opposite tale Frank Jury had told everyone. Jury had been treated like a returning war hero. Free drinks, food and back-slapping congratulations met him everyplace he went. Now people began to think he was either a fool or, worse, a bald-faced liar. Even his old friends started avoiding him.

Talk of the good citizens of Eagle Buttes getting even with the Shoshones soon began to fade away. No one was going to mount up and ride off into the Tobacco Root Mountains to fight the powerful Shoshones; that was a job for the troopers at Fort Pakston. They were paid to risk their lives, local folks were not. At the height of the endless speculation, a small band of cavalry men from the fort rode into town, led by Sergeant Cleary, to buy much-needed supplies because the army wagon had not shown up as scheduled. The sergeant commanded half a dozen mounted men to safely escort the new supplies back to Pakston, in the four-mule team pulling their wagon.

Cleary was quick to hear about the murderous ambush by the Shoshones in the Tobacco Root Mountains. He was directed to the sheriff's office when he asked for details. Cas Wickman denied any knowledge of what happened and told Cleary to go to Doctor Caldwell's office and talk directly to R.T. Sturgis, if he was in any condition to talk at all. When Jury heard soldier boys were in town from Fort Pakston, he immediately panicked, staying off the streets out of sight. Sergeant Cleary was the last man he wanted questioning

81

him after the dangerous rifle deal he'd made with the Crows.

The sergeant found Sturgis at the doctor's house, asking Caldwell if he could talk to his patient briefly. The doctor informed him R.T. was still weak and struggling to stay alive, so he'd give him only a few moments because of the gravity of his condition. He led the cavalryman down the hall into Sturgis's small room, where he lay asleep. One look was all Cleary needed to see how badly broken and bloody the man was. His face and arms were covered in cuts and dark, black bruises, his closed eyes reduced to two, black swollen slits.

Doctor Caldwell leaned down and whispered in R.T.'s ear. 'Mr Sturgis . . . you have an important visitor . . . can you talk for a few moments?'

R.T.'s eyes opened just far enough to make out the blurry image of a blue uniform with yellow chevrons on the sleeve. Even in his precarious physical condition, he knew enough not to answer any questions about the savage ambush and why he'd hired men to ride into the mountains in the first place. Cleary's first question was how many men he took with him into the mountains.

Sturgis swallowed hard and, wetting his lips, tried to speak. Doctor Caldwell quickly saw his discomfort and, reaching for the small night stand next to the bed, poured a half glass of water from a pitcher. Lifting R.T.'s head, he let him take a few sips, before he tried again.

'I had . . . maybe nine . . . or ten men.' He laid back down, closing his eyes and grimacing.

'Do you think anyone else got out besides you?

Anyone else I could question?' R.T. only shook his head, knowing it was a lie.

'Can you tell me why you were even in that part of the mountains? You had to know it's all Shoshone country.'

'I was . . . prospecting for gold.'

'Gold, in the Tobacco Root Mountains? I've never heard of any real strike in there. Farther south I know there are a few small mines, but not that high up.'

Sturgis didn't answer this time. He shrugged once. He was done talking.

The doctor tugged at Cleary's sleeve, motioning him toward the door. Once out in the hall after closing the door, he added one more piece of information about his patient's disastrous journey.

'You asked if anyone else got out alive. One other man I know of did. His name is Frank Jury. You might want to talk to him to get a few more answers.'

The sergeant's eyes narrowed. That name sounded familiar. He tried to remember where he had heard it before. Then it came to him; Jury was one of the wagon men that came to the fort sometime back to trade with the Crow Indians.

'I think I might have already met him,' he answered. 'Do you know where I can find him?'

'Either down at the sheriff's office, he's friends with Cas Wickman, or possibly in Mr Sturgis's office across the street. He worked for him, but I'm not really sure where he lives.'

'Thank you, doctor. I appreciate your help, and hope Mr Sturgis gets better before I leave to go back to the fort. There are still some things I'd like him to answer when he's in a more stable frame of mind.'

Later that evening, after businesses had closed and locked their doors and coal oil lamps were out, only the saloons and gambling parlours up and down the street showed any sight or sound of men who didn't care what time it was. Doctor Caldwell's house at the far end of town stood dark and quiet. The doctor and his wife, Ophelia, were already asleep. Down the hall in his room, R.T. Sturgis steeled himself against the pain, slowly pulling himself up, inch by inch, and stuffing pillows behind his back for support so he could sit up in bed. Cleary's visit troubled him. The last thing he needed now was military people poking around. He took in a long, deep breath, trying to relax and think all this over. Far down the street he could hear the tiny sounds of laughter and a piano playing as revellers took on another night. Moments later he heard another sound that made him sit back up, listening closer. It was the whisper of someone's clothes brushing up against the wooden clapboard siding right outside. He stopped breathing. There it was again, causing the hair on the back of his neck to tingle with fear. R.T.'s hand reached for the drawer in the nightstand. Quietly opening it, he slowly pulled out his pistol, the only personal thing found on him when he crawled out of the mountains. The big iron was heavy in his weakened hands. It took both hands just to cock the hammer full back as he shifted in the bed to face the partially opened window across the room. Suddenly, the black shadow of a man filled the window frame. Pulling up the sash with one hand while holding a six-gun in the other, the assassin started to lean through the window. Sturgis's trembling hands levelled his pistol with both hands, firing one thundering shot. The blinding flash of gunpowder briefly lit the room, the recoil of the pistol spinning the weapon from his hands, before everything went dark again. R.T. fell back on the bed yelling for help.

Down the hall, Caldwell and his wife sat straight up in bed. He fumbled for the lamp on the table next to the bed. Finding it, he got it lit. 'You stay here while I go see what happened!' he ordered Ophelia. 'Lock the door until I get back.'

'But Nelson . . . you don't even have a gun for protection. Don't leave this room until help comes. There's no telling what you might find in there!'

'I can't wait for help. I've got to see if Mr Sturgis is all right or not. Now just do what I say, hon. I'll be back quick as I can.'

At R.T.'s door, Caldwell slowly twisted the handle before peeking inside. The room was dark, but he could hear Sturgis breathing heavily. It took a moment for his eyes to adjust to the dark. Stepping all the way in, he went to the bed helping to prop up Sturgis, who was still sitting up. The room reeked of burnt gunpowder.

'What in God's name happened? Did you fire that shot or someone else?'

'I'm OK . . . someone came up outside to . . . kill me . . . look out there. I think I got him before he had the chance.'

The doctor went to the window, cautiously sticking his head out far enough to see the crumpled body of Frank Jury lying face up, a neat, round bullet hole in his forehead. His eyes bulged wide open, but saw nothing. Sturgis's lucky shot in the dark and its .45 calibre bullet had done its work instantly and completely. Frank Jury, the town hero turned midnight assassin, would never see another sunrise over Eagle Buttes. He died along with his lies, and was quickly buried the next day.

Word of Jury's killing and by whom spread throughout town like wildfire, spawning endless questions without answers. News of it reached Sergeant Cleary the next morning as he stood watching his wagon being loaded on the supply dock in back of Sirius Weems' dry goods store. Weems and the sergeant were standing together when someone came up with the story. Cleary's jaw dropped, but he also made a quick decision in the same instant. He ordered one of his men to take the loading list and continue checking off items, while he went back to Doctor Caldwell's house to talk to his star patient again.

R.T. was sitting up in bed when the doctor escorted Cleary into the bedroom. One look from Sturgis was all it took to make it clear he was not happy about his return visitor. The sergeant appraised Sturgis a moment before speaking.

'I know your condition makes it difficult for you to answer more questions, but I just heard about this shooting last night and had to see you one last time before I leave town. What you can tell me could have a strong bearing to my superior officer, Captain

Rutherford, once I get back to Fort Pakston. This Indian uprising you became involved in could grow into a lot more trouble for whites all over the territory, if they decide to go on a war party. Your trip into their country could be the reason it might start. First of all, do you have any idea why this man Frank Jury, who worked for you, would try to kill you?'

'I have . . . none.' Sturgis slowly shook his head, carefully measuring his words. 'All I know for sure . . . he came to that window with a gun in his hand. I didn't have . . . any time to ask him why.'

'How well did you know him? Were you friends or had you done any kind of business deals with him?'

'No, he worked for me . . . that's all there was to it.'

'In what capacity did he work for you?'

The pained expression on R.T.'s face only grew more obvious. 'I sometimes had him run my wagons . . . out of town . . . in town, whatever I needed done.'

'Are you saying there were no hard feelings between the two of you? He must have had something to try and kill you in your bed?'

'I'm saying I don't know why?'

'Did you owe him any money, anything like that?'

'Just whatever wages he had coming . . . it wasn't much.'

Cleary paused, thinking the answers over. He was getting nowhere, and Sturgis wasn't about to help him either.

'One final question before I go. When you were attacked by the Shoshone, did you see how many of them came at you? Ten, fifteen, maybe more?'

'I didn't have time to count. They were . . . in hiding at the top of the trail. Halfway up, all hell broke loose. They rode down on us killing everyone still . . . alive. I'm lucky I ever made it back here. That's all I can remember.'

'All right, I'll put all this in my report. Thank you for the added information. I hope you recover soon. Goodbye, Mr Sturgis.'

Cleary and the doctor left the room, closing the door behind them. The smallest smile of satisfaction creased R.T.'s cut and bruised face. He sank back into the soft feathered pillows. He'd kept his golden secret, and dead men told no tales. The only thing left that might be trouble was whether or not Zack Hitch made it back alive. He'd seen him kicking his horse into timber when the slaughter was going on. Once he got back up on his feet, he'd have to get the answer to that final question. The days and weeks he'd spent pitifully dragging himself out of the mountains now seemed to be all worth it. Fate had favoured him in an extraordinary way. But fate can also be a fickle lady who turns a dark face against you in the blink of her eye. Zack Hitch just might be the one man who could convince her to do it.

SEVEN

Cas Wickman began visiting his boss at the doctor's house after Cleary and his men rode out of town for Fort Pakston. Wickman didn't have the brass or backbone Frank Jury did. He'd spent his days worrying about the spreading word of the Shoshone ambush and why it happened, plus now Jury's killing by Sturgis. R.T.'s name seemed to be wrapped up in all these troubles. His boss had always paid to have his dirty work done, whether it was the beating of someone in an alley or the pull of a trigger, by men like Hoyt and Jury. Now that had changed. The sheriff began wondering if Sturgis could actually do any killing himself. That thought made Wickman begin to fear the man he worked for, if it came down to just the two of them to survive further troubles. On one visit, the moment Doctor Caldwell left the room R.T. began questioning Cas.

'I want to know what happened to Jury that he got so desperate he tried to kill me?' Sturgis sat straight up in bed, staring hard-eyed at his paid lawman.

'How would I know? He must have went crazy or something to try that. I didn't believe it even when people came down to my office next morning telling me about it,' Cass lied through his teeth.

'He never expected me to make it out of the mountains and tried to finish me off himself, is what I think. The only thing I'm sure of now is he won't get a second chance!'

'He sure as hell won't. You saw to that. When does Caldwell think he'll let you out of here?'

'He says maybe this week, but I'm going to try to make it shorter if I can. I've got business matters to take care of, and a lot of other things to get out of the way. I can't do that lying in here on my back. By the way, have you seen Zack Hitch around town since all this took place?'

'Hitch? No, last time I saw him was when all of you rode out of town to head into the mountains. Do you think he made it back, too?'

'I'm not certain if he got out or not. That's why I asked. It's important for me to find out, though.'

'I can ride out to his place if I can find it and see if he's around. If he survived, he sure hasn't shown himself here.'

'No, don't you go out there. I'll do that myself once I get back on my feet. I don't want to put the spook on him asking too many questions. He might pack up and run for it. You know how squirrelly those backwoods loners can be. Stay away from him. That's an order!'

Jesper Tubbs worked on his golden ledge each day,

growing more troubled by the tragic events of the last few weeks. It was bad enough that white men from town had come searching for him, but their slaughter at the hands of Standing Bear was even worse. He knew it could trigger a cavalry response to bring in large numbers of troopers to find the Shoshone village and destroy it in an all-out battle. Even if that didn't happen, he was certain more white men would try to find him by any means. He couldn't shake the dark thoughts from his mind, no matter how hard he tried.

He put down his rock hammer. Sitting on his heels, he ran both hands through his thickly matted, white-streaked hair. Closing his eyes, he tried for the hundredth time to think things through for answers that could make some sense. He kept coming back to the same thing. He and he alone had created the deadly situation through his discovery of the golden ledge. There was no two ways about it. And now he had to take more ore out of the mountains to have it crushed and assayed again. There was no way he could go back to Eagle Buttes to do so. That was out of the question. He had heard there was another small stamp mill in Oro Fino, but that ride was twice as far as Eagle Buttes. Yet he had no choice.

Struggling with all this, he also worried Standing Bear might ride in again and tell him he had to leave the mountains for good. He'd almost done so last time he saw the chief. The long ride out to Oro Fino sounded even better with that possibility. If he wasn't in camp, Standing Bear would have to wait until he returned. Maybe more time would favour his staying.

He realized through all this he'd become a victim of his own circumstances. He never imagined things could get this bad but they had and could even grow worse. He'd found a fabulously rich gold strike but could not develop it to its fullest potential. He was severely limited on the small amount of ore he could pack out on Jerry's back. In his lowest moments he almost wished he'd never found the golden ridge at all. He got to his feet, looking at Jenny.

'Come on, old girl. Let's head for camp. I've got me more thinking to do.'

At Fort Pakston that very same evening, Captain Ryder adjusted the coal oil lamp hanging over his desk, beginning to study a large field map atop it. Sergeant Cleary was stood to one side, looking on, with Lieutenant Mark Wheeler on the other, when Ryder stabbed a finger down on the map.

'That, gentlemen, is where I believe the Shoshone summer camp is located. And it matches where the Crows say they are, too. Red Moccasin said they have at least one hundred teepees and a large remuda of horses. I don't quite believe that, we all know how Indians exaggerate things. But I have no doubt their camp is a big one. If I go in after them I'd want both Red Moccasin and Blue Swallow to scout for us leading the way. What do you say to my plans, lieutenant?'

This was Wheeler's first field assignment outside of his original deployment at Fort Atkinson, in Kansas, where he worked mostly at a desk. The thought of a military battle against Indians was exciting and adventurous. He answered with obvious enthusiasm.

'I'd say you have a great plan, sir. From what I've heard, the Shoshones are only armed with bows and arrows plus a few old, single-shot muskets. We should be able to ride right over the top of those hostiles and bring them down.' He grinned ear to ear at the prospect of a quick victory to go on his military record.

'And what about you, Sergeant Cleary? What are your thoughts on all this?'

'I'd have to say any cavalry outfit riding into a Shoshone stronghold like that is going to be known about long before they got there. That means the Indians can choose the time and place to attack. That's a big edge to have. It also might give them another advantage in numbers, even if they can't field as many men as we can.'

'And how would that be possible?' Ryder pressed for more.

'Three or four dozen Shoshones fighting from cover can easily match twice that number of mounted cavalrymen riding out in the open. Not only that, they'd take fewer casualties than we would. I remember what happened to Captain Bettencourt down south when he chased a small band of Apaches who were really only decoys. They drew him and his men into a waiting ambush by a force no larger than his. Bettencourt was killed and so were all sixty of his men.'

'You are correct, sergeant. Are you listening and learning, Mr Wheeler?' Ryder turned to the embarrassed young officer, who realized he'd been trumped by a man of lesser rank but far more field experience.

The lieutenant nodded without speaking.

Ryder decided to ease his embarrassment by changing the subject. 'When this engagement against the Shoshones is over, we're riding for Eagle Buttes. I want to talk to this man R.T. Sturgis I've heard so much about. It's beginning to sound to me as if he has some serious explaining to do. Why the local sheriff there hasn't looked into this and done some questioning on his own is something else I don't quite understand. From what you've told me, Mr Cleary, none of his story makes any sense either. This cock and bull story by Sturgis that he hired a group of men just to go into the mountains on the chance they'd go prospecting for gold is another senseless lie as far as I'm concerned. First thing first, though. We'll take on the Shoshones as soon as I get the men I've requested from Fort Laramie. I want to be certain we have sufficient numbers of troopers to take on Standing Bear. And I'll use 12-pounder field howitzers to break down his resistance even before we ride in and fire a single shot.'

While Captain Ryder bided his time waiting for reinforcements to arrive, R.T. Sturgis was finally allowed to get back on his feet, leaving Doctor Caldwell's care, although he was forced to walk with the use of a cane to steady himself. His normally domineering attitude only grew worse because of it. Not only was normal walking painful and difficult, but he quickly learned he could not longer mount a horse without two men boosting him up in the saddle. Even then, the pain and discomfort were too great to make it worth doing. Instead, he had to rely on a horse and buggy to get around. For his first two weeks back in office, he stayed mostly at his desk working on a backlog of paperwork, but the gnawing concern over whether or not Zack Hitch had made it back alive never left his mind. The old tracker might be the only other man left alive that really knew what happened and why on their ill-fated trip into the Tobacco Root Mountains. Early one afternoon Sturgis decided he could wait no longer. It was time to answer that nagging question. R.T. was not a man who left messy details hanging. Hitch was one of them.

'Where are you going, boss?' Wickman helped R.T. up into the buggy.

'Just a little ride to get some fresh air and get away from all that paperwork on my desk,' he insisted, knowing it was a lie.

'Want me to ride along for company? I wouldn't mind getting out of town for a while either.'

'No, I do not. You stay here and keep your eyes open. That's what I'm paying you for. I'll be back in a while.' He settled a small, black leather satchel on the seat next to him.

'All right,' the sheriff nodded. 'I just thought I'd ask.'

'I'm not paying you to think. I'm paying you to do what I tell you, and don't forget it.'

Sturgis snapped the reins down and the buggy rattled forward down the street until it disappeared at the far end out of town. He thought he knew the general area where Hitch's cabin was supposed to be located, even though he'd never been out there. The wagon bounced down one timbered road after another for nearly two hours before finally breaking to a halt in a small clearing. The old log cabin stood in the deep shade of tall pines, a small twist of smoke curling up from its stone chimney. Out back, Sturgis could see a pole corral with a lean-to shed. A horse and mule stood with their ears pitched forward at the new arrivals. He paused a moment, taking it all in, before calling out.

'Hitch, you in there? Come on out. It's me, Sturgis. I've got the rest of the money I owe you. Come get it!'

A long, eerie silence followed before the cabin door opened ever so slowly, just far enough for Zack to peek out.

'I've got your cash right here in my satchel.' Sturgis held up the bag. 'I'm too stove in to get down. You'll have to fetch it.'

The trapper stepped outside and stopped, but with a shotgun in his hands. Standing for a moment, he tried sizing up his sudden uninvited guest. Sturgis waved the bag temptingly. Hitch started forward, tucking the shotgun under one arm for quick use if he needed it.

'What have you got the shotgun for?' R.T. questioned. 'There's no need for that. All I came out here for is to pay up so we're even.'

Reaching the buggy, Hitch spoke for the first time. 'It took you long enough to do it. Put the money on the seat, and keep your hands where I can see 'em.'

Sturgis opened the satchel, taking out a roll of bills neatly wrapped in a red paper band. 'Here, this makes us even. Now put that damn shotgun down will you?

Haven't you figured out you can trust me after what we've both been through?'

Hitch took the money with one hand, stuffing it into his pants pocket. 'Trust you?' he questioned. 'I heard about Frank Jury and how you shot him down. Sorta' strange anyone who wasn't killed off by them Indians dies once he gets back here, ain't it?'

'Jury tried to kill me in my bed. I had to defend myself. What would you do, lay there and get murdered!'

'It don't matter none what I'd have done. I've got my money. Now turn that buggy around and git out of here. We got no more dealin' to do with each other. You led all those men into that slaughter because you wouldn't listen to me when I tried to warn you. You're a thick-headed fool. As far as I'm concerned, you're just as bad as them Shoshones for all the killin' that took place. Go on, git!'

R.T. reached for the reins as Hitch backed away from the buggy, still facing him while holding the shotgun. Safely at the cabin door, he turned to go inside. In that same instant Sturgis reached into the satchel, pulling out his black-barreled .36 calibre pistol and firing three shots as fast as he could pull the trigger. The bullets' impact drove the old tracker through the door and onto the floor face down. He moaned in pain, trying to pull himself away, then relaxed in death.

Sturgis painfully exited the buggy. Inside the cabin, he knelt and retrieved the money from Hitch's pocket. Struggling to stand again, he looked around the dingy interior. A coal oil lamp stood on a table nearby.

Removing the mantle, he splashed the liquid across the floor until it was empty. Stepping back outside, he lit a stick match before tossing it into the room. A sudden swoosh of flames danced across the floor, lighting the room in a fiery glow. By the time Sturgis reached the buggy and pulled himself up into it, the cabin walls were cracking with sheets of fire as the inferno grew to a roar. His horse jittered in fear, jerking in its traces. Turning the buggy around to leave, R.T. took one last look back over his shoulder, the entire cabin now engulfed in flames.

Now there was no one left to tell the tale of the slaughter in the Tobacco Root Mountains but Sturgis himself, and he had no intention whatsoever of doing that. He had also become the killer of two men with no guilty conscience about either one. In fact, he had to admit to himself that killing got easier the more he did of it. Once back in Eagle Buttes, someone on the street called out to Sturgis as his buggy rolled by, pointing at the black smudge of smoke rising in the sky several miles away. No one would ever know it was the funeral pyre engulfing the last remains of Zack Hitch, but R.T. Sturgis. And he was completely satisfied with the results of his treachery.

Several days later two men out hunting discovered the burned out remains of the cabin and the charred remains of Hitch's body. It was assumed by everyone in town who heard about it that the backwoods loner had likely died by his own hand after falling asleep while smoking in bed. Lady Luck still smiled down on R.T. Sturgis. He'd gotten away with bloody murder twice. The only man left with deep, personal knowledge of

R.T.'s ill-fated trip into the Tobacco Root Mountains, was Cas Wickman.

The nervous sheriff had already begun worrying if he was number three on his boss's list. In every conversation he had with Sturgis, regardless of the subject, he searched for some hidden meaning or hint he was being set up for a sudden departure. He tried making contact with R.T. as little as possible, but that was a struggle on a day to day basis. Cas knew he was no fast-draw lawman or respected pillar of justice in Eagle Buttes. He's never fired a shot at anyone in his entire life, let alone as sheriff. He could lock up drunks and threaten people, but it was Sturgis who pinned the badge on him, and Sturgis whose law he was enforcing. He felt hemmed in with no way out.

Many miles and days away, Captain Rutherford L. Ryder stepped outside his office onto the front porch at Fort Pakston to the call of his orderly. Entering the front gate, he saw a line of fresh, new troopers, forty in number, followed by two mule-drawn wagons. One carried the pair of 12-pounder mountain howitzers and shells broken down for easy packing, the other food and supplies to feed the troops on their long journey up from Fort Laramie.

'They're fine-looking soldiers, aren't they sir?' the young trooper exclaimed, watching the riders beginning to fill the compound.

'That they are, private. And I hope they can fight as good as they look, because I know the Shoshone will. Those new howitzers will give Standing Bear a taste of what I mean to do to him. No medicine man's magic mumbo jumbo is going to stop me.'

Private Granger did not answer. He knew overwhelming the Shoshone stronghold would not be easy, even with the howitzers. Standing Bear had beaten back previous attempts to subdue him before he took his people deep into the Tobacco Root Mountains for refuge. He'd refused to sign peace treaties years earlier after watching tribes that did, only to see their ancestral lands invaded by white men seeking gold and silver, or timber interests, and settlers. Even the United States Army had done their share of it, for reasons no Indian could understand. Now there was nothing left to sign or bargain over. The cavalry plan was straightforward: surrender or die. You did not have to hold the rank of captain to know that Standing Bear would never surrender.

The new cavalrymen riding into Fort Pakston were led by Lieutenant Austin P. Trivette, who had some field experience corralling the Lakota Indians and their chief Red Cloud farther south. At his first meeting with Ryder, after settling his men, the captain made Sergeant Cleary Trivette's immediate aide because of his knowledge of the surrounding country and supposed location of the Shoshone summer village, nearly a week's ride away. Over the next six busy days the new arrivals were integrated into Ryder's command and plans for the attack. Finally satisfied the entire force could work as one unit, they were ordered to move out. Two other notable men flanked Captain Ryder, Trivette and Cleary, as they led the long column of troopers outside the gate of Fort Pakston that day. Neither wore a uniform. Red Moccasin and Blue Swallow were the main trackers who knew the way to the Shoshone village. Crow elders had their own reasons for allowing the pair to help the white horse soldiers. The Shoshone were old enemies whose lands they coveted for their own. The cavalry meant to break Standing Bear's grip on that high country. Now the Crow scouts would serve two important purposes.

Jesper Tubbs could not imagine the powerful forces far away that were moving inexorably toward a murderous showdown battle. His worry was that Standing Bear would ride in one day to tell him he had to leave his mountain home, never to return. Yet, when long shadows of evening bathed his camp each day, no Shoshones came. He'd breathe another sigh of relief, until he finally decided to pack up his ore and begin the long trip to Oro Fino and its stamp mill. A squawking blue jay woke him early on the morning of his departure. The Indians always said the cocky blue bird that made so much noise was a busybody who could tell wild tales of things happening far away. Jesper sat up from under his thin wool blanket, watching the little flyer hopping around camp looking for scraps of food.

'Well, do you have something to tell me?' he asked, the jay suddenly flying up onto a tree branch and looking down scolding him. 'I guess not.' He shook his head. 'Someone once told me no news is good news, so I'll settle for that. Anyway, it's time for me to pack up Jenny and head out.'

EIGHT

Captain Ryder and his long line of cavalrymen arrived several miles away from the Shoshone village late in the afternoon of their eight-day march. The timing fit perfectly with his plans. He gathered Trivette and Cleary around with specific orders he wanted followed without question.

'I want no fires of any kind tonight. The men can eat a cold meal. I also want all horses roped on a picket line with guards watching over them so none wander away. If even one got loose it would likely head for the Shoshone *remuda* and give our advantage of surprise away. I'd personally court martial any man that lets that happen. Lieutenant, I want you to take half the men along with Sergeant Cleary and Blue Swallow to lead you plus one of the howitzers around the far side of the village while remaining out of sight. Red Moccasin will stay here with me. At the first hint of good light, I'll open up with our 12-pounder. Soon as you hear it, immediately begin firing, too. Concentrate your fire on the Shoshone *remuda*. I'll direct ours on the village.

Without their horses, none of these savages can get away. I want ten full rounds fired as fast as you can load and light. After the ten, mount your men and ride into the village, shooting anything and everyone that moves. We'll be coming in from the opposite direction and have them in a crossfire, closing the jaws on our trap. Are there any questions? If so let's hear them now so we're all clear on exactly what we're supposed to do and when.'

'Do you intend to take any prisoners back to the fort?' Trivette asked.

'I do not. I want every single one of them dead. Standing Bear had his chance to move his people to a reservation. He refused and fled. Now he'll pay the full price for his stubborn resistance, and it will be a great lesson for any others who try that.'

'You don't mean women and children too, do you?' the lieutenant questioned.

'I said all of them, Mr Trivette.'

The officer looked to Sergeant Cleary, who said nothing, only staring back with a blank expression on his face.

'Sir, I've never shot down unarmed women and children. Surely you can't mean an order like that, do you?'

'I mean every word of it. Just follow my orders and do your job, Mr Trivette. Today might be a new experience for you, but I'm sure your conscience will clear up once we have our victory in hand. And your military record will also be enhanced by doing so.'

A chilly morning dawned with grey stringers of low clouds still nestled in the timber-lined valleys and basins. The long line of teepees in the village stood quiet and still, a few thin wisps of smoke drifting up from last night's cooking fires. A skinny camp dog slowly got to his feet, stretching out the kinks and shivering in the icy air. The cur suddenly turned toward timber beyond the village, testing the air with his nose. The hair on his neck stood up, a low, menacing growl growing in his throat as the first strange scent of intruders drifted in on morning air. His growl became a bark, the bark a loud howl, as more camp dogs ran up to join the mongrel's chorus.

A young brave sleepily exited a nearby teepee, scowling at the noisy animals that woke him. Picking up a stone, he hurled it, hitting one offending animal with a howl of pain. Before the Shoshone could turn back to enter his teepee, an explosive 'BOOM!' shattered the still mountain air, the projectile landing squarely in the village and cutting through teepees and men, women and children in them. Before that sound faded away a second deadly missile whistled in, exploding among the horses in the meadow at the back of the village, killing and maiming its first victims. Bewildered Indians ran wild-eyed from teepees, rifles in hand, trying to make some sense of the sudden, unexpected attack but found no enemy to engage.

More howitzers boomed out of sight in timber as shells fell in flashes of fire and killing shrapnel. The murderous barrage went on until it seemed it would never end then suddenly stopped, followed by a bugle charge from Ryder's mounted cavalrymen riding full tilt out of timber directly for the village and firing with pistols and rifles as they came in. Just as the captain's men reached the teepees, Trivette's troopers charged in from the opposite direction, their shooting and shouting catching the confused Shoshones in a withering crossfire.

Standing Bear crawled out from his shattered teepee, bloody and wounded, still gripping his precious Henry rifle. Looking up, he saw Trivette leading his men coming straight at him. Riding at the officer's side was Blue Swallow, yelling a war cry and firing his pistol. Both men saw each other at the same instant. Standing Bear pulled himself to his feet. Lifting the rifle, he aimed at the traitor who had shown the white soldiers the way to his village. Both fired simultaneously, Blue Swallow's horse crashing to the ground struck full in the chest and throwing the Crow rider through the air, landing nearly at the chief's feet. Instantly, Standing Bear hurled himself atop the Crow, pinning him while he pulled out his razor-sharp knife and plunged it down again and again as Blue Swallow screamed and twisted under him, until he could scream no more. The chief almost made it back up to his feet but more bullets tore into him, spinning him back down dead atop his hated enemy. The sudden and savage overwhelming surprise attack completely decimated the village, with bodies scattered across the ground in every direction.

Captain Ryder wheeled his horse around in a circle, still holding a smoking hot pistol in his hand, taking in his victory, as Sergeant Cleary rode up alongside him.

'Sergeant, take some men and finish off anyone and any horses still left alive. I don't want the chance someone can crawl away and get on a horse. After that, you and Trivette burn everything still left standing to the ground.'

'Yes sir!' Cleary saluted, waving over several troopers and ordering them to follow him.

Lieutenant Trivette appeared out of the smoke and carnage, his captain waving him over. 'You did good work, lieutenant. Both you and your men are to be congratulated.' A grim smile spread across Ryder's face. 'These savages never knew what hit them. My plan was perfectly executed. Now you can see why carrying out orders, whether you agree with them or not, is so important to complete success. Have you had the chance yet to see if we have any lost or wounded men?'

'I only did a quick count, sir. It looked like I may have two men killed, and five more wounded. Those Henry rifles the Shoshone were using is the reason why.'

'Yes, those damn rifles. I noticed that too, but I haven't had the time to check on my own men yet. I think it will only be a small number. We'll take our dead back with us for the Christian burial they deserve. They've served their country and this command proudly. The Shoshones can be left where they fell. They deserve nothing better. Before we ride out of here I also want a complete count of the Indians killed, men, women and children. Command back at Fort Laramie will want an accurate number of our success here today, aside from my own personal notes and explanations. One other thing. Any teepees still left standing I want burned to the ground. I want nothing left here to show there ever was a Shoshone village. Time will take care of the rest.'

As Ryder finished his orders, the muted sound of a baby crying came from one of the teepees still standing nearby. The captain twisted in the saddle, cocking his head to hear the infant squall again. 'There's someone still alive in there,' he waved his pistol at the teepee. 'Go in and put an end to that noise, lieutenant.'

'But sir . . .' Trivette grimaced at the order. 'It sounds like only a child. For the love of God, is that what our mission here is really all about? Don't we have even a shred of compassion for a baby? That would be simple murder.'

'You are a cavalry officer, Mr Trivette. I expect you to act like one and carry out an order when it's given by a superior officer, not question it like some whimpering schoolboy. I would suggest you do so now, or when I write my report on this engagement your refusal to do will be foremost in it!'

The two men stared hard at each other for several seconds longer as Trivette struggled with indecision. 'I'm waiting for you to carry out my order, Mr Trivette. Do so now or I'll relieve you of your command and weapons here and now!' Ryder's voice rose in red-faced anger with a threat he had every intention of carrying out.

The lieutenant broke his stare, slowly getting down from his horse. Walking to the teepee, he turned and looked up at the captain one more time. His stare remained steady and resolute. Trivette pulled the entrance flap back, stepping inside. The grisly smell of death instantly assaulted him. Shrapnel holes in the skin covering of the teepee allowed in just enough light that he could make out the forms of bodies sprawled across the floor. An old, grey-haired man lay curled up at his feet. Next to him a young boy who appeared to be a teenager had his hand draped over the old man. Up against the teepee wall, a middle-aged women with long, black braided hair, was curled up in death, protecting the body of her baby still kicking and crying for her. Lieutenant Trivette stepped closer, carefully rolling the woman's body off the little infant. He stared down at the child, thinking briefly about his own two young daughters and wife back east, safe and sound from all this killing. He wondered how anyone could call this helpless baby the enemy of anyone. Didn't it have the right to live just like anyone else, white or Indian? Suddenly Captain Ryder's loud voice ended his troubled questioning.

'Mr Trivette, what are you waiting for? Get on with it, sir. Do your job, or I'll come in there and do it myself!'

The young officer pulled his pistol, still staring down at the fussing infant. He noticed a small rawhide chewy obviously used as a pacifier. Putting it in the baby's mouth, he prayed it would stop crying, before pulling a heavy fur blanket over the top and covering the child up. Aiming the pistol down away from the little bundle, he fired one thudding shot into the floor, quickly exiting the teepee.

Outside he pulled himself up into the saddle without looking at Ryder. 'Very good, lieutenant,' the captain said. 'You'll learn that a cavalry officer may have to do a number of things from time to time he might find distasteful, but that's part of wearing this uniform. Today was one of those days. I would suggest you not dwell on it.'

The wagons were brought into the village, loading up dead and wounded troopers who could not ride on their own. Both Ryder and Cleary made a count of the Henry rifles found among the dead Shoshones. The captain hefted one of the rifles in his hand, looking over at Cleary.

'How do you suppose they got their hands on these?' he questioned. 'They're newer and better than our own army issue.'

'I don't know sir, but they had a number of them. Just about every warrior we found had one. I'm sure it must be a treasonous offence to sell them to Indians, serious enough to hang for, or at least a long prison sentence.'

'Indeed it is, Mr Cleary. And once we get back to the fort and take care of our own people, we're going to look into it and find out who was responsible for the death of our men. I'll see to it personally, and you will help me. You have my promise on it.'

Before the long line of mounted troopers and wagons rode out of the smoldering remains of the village, Captain Ryder already had a new name to add to his field map of the Tobacco Root Mountains. This place of surprise and slaughter would be called Massacre Meadow, to commemorate the cavalry's overwhelming victory over the troublesome Shoshone Indians and their chief. The lure of death and dead bodies would feed wolves and grizzly bears for weeks to come. In the end all that would remain would be bleached white bones.

Jesper Tubbs made the long trip to Oro Fino and its stamp mill to have his ore processed and collect the money paid in gold and silver coins. He left town with bulging packsacks of food and money to a flurry of people wondering where his rich strike was, exactly as the case had been in Eagle Buttes. However, Oro Fino was much smaller and had no one running roughshod over it like R.T. Sturgis. The strange old man quickly vanished back into the mountains, noticing he'd made the journey in less time than he'd originally thought. Back at his camp, he decided enough time had passed to take the chance and ride to the Shoshone village and see if Standing Bear would still allow his presence in the mountains. It had worried him throughout his entire trip to Oro Fino. Now he was ready to face the answer from his old friend. After a couple of days' settling camp, he saddled up Jenny to make the ride the following morning.

Tubbs rode easily over familiar ground along mountain game trails through whispering pines streaked in shafts of afternoon sunlight. It was a beautiful day. Then everything suddenly changed. Before reaching the village near sundown, a gentle breeze carried the unmistakable odour of death. Jesper pulled to a halt, straining to see ahead near the horse meadow. He could not. Urging Jenny forward, he pulled his old, single-shot rifle from its skin scabbard, laying the long gun across his lap in case he needed it quickly. Exiting trees, he stopped again. The scene that met his eyes was so unreal he had to squint, trying a second time to take it in. Boney remains of horses lay scattered in various stages of decay; the village beyond a skeleton of blackened teepee poles burned to the ground. A breath caught in the old man's throat. A dozen large grey wolves wandered from one body to another, devouring the grisly remains. Jesper's face twisted in revulsion. He leaped off Jenny, firing one long, desperate shot across the meadow and sending the four-legged monsters running for timber out of sight. He was almost afraid to go closer, yet he had to see what happened. Back atop the big mule, he kicked her forward.

Entering where the village had stood, remains of Shoshone men, women and children lay scattered, twisted in death. The enormity of it was so overwhelming it forced Tubbs to dismount, holding onto the saddle to steady himself. He pulled up his neck scarf over his nose, trying to keep back the stench. Tears of despair rolled down his whiskered face and he cried out loud for the first time since he was a little boy. He could not understand what had happened, and how men could do this to each other, no matter the colour of their skin. Empty brass cartridges lay scattered everywhere he looked across ground, chopped up with crisscrossing tracks of running horses. One look at the shell casings made it clear it was the cavalry who had initiated the slaughter.

Jesper wandered through the remains up to the only teepee still standing. He wondered if he dared look inside. Every emotion told him to saddle up and get as far away from here as fast as he could, yet he lingered for some reason. Taking a few steps toward it, he thought he heard a small whimper and came to a stop. Surely, it had to be the breeze whispering through teepee poles. Cupping one hand to his ear, he listened harder. There it was again. Forcing himself forward, he carefully pulled back the teepee flap. The hot rush of putrid air from inside forced him to step back. Pinching the scarf over his nose, he stepped inside. Scattered light revealed the outline of dead bodies. Stepping over an old man and a boy, he saw a small movement under a blanket, next to the body of a woman. Jesper kneeled, slowly pulling the blanket back and revealing the round, brown face of a baby, eyes closed, struggling to breathe and cry.

He recoiled violently, nearly falling over backwards. How had this child survived? That couldn't be possible, yet somehow it had. There was nothing he could do to save it. Yet he could not turn away and leave. His mind swirled with wild ideas and indecision. He couldn't take the child and leave. That was completely out of the question. He tried pulling his hand back. A little brown hand suddenly found his fingers, gripping them tightly. Jesper wiped sweat off his forehead with his free hand, still transfixed on the little child. He began explaining out loud why he couldn't save it. He knew nothing about children, let alone a baby. There was no way it could survive, living with him in his meagre mountain camp. He kept on arguing several minutes longer until finally he exited the teepee with a blanket-wrapped bundle in his arms. Jesper Tubbs had just become a father after every instinct had told him that otherwise the little child would surely die. He could not bring himself to add to the death already surrounding him.

Back atop Jenny, Tubbs urged his mule quickly across the meadow away from this place of death and ghastly images. Retrieving his canteen, he opened the spout and splashed a bit of water into his cupped hand, slowly trickling it into the baby's mouth. The little boy child eagerly sucked it down. Jesper repeated it again with the same results. The old prospector had another idea. Pulling a dried plug of venison from his jacket pocket, he pinched off a piece and put it in his mouth, chewing it until it became wet and pulpy. Twisting off a smaller piece, he touched the baby's lips with it. Instantly, little jaws began chewing on it before swallowing. Jesper repeated it again with the same results. The baby was nearly starved to death. As the child gummed down its third piece, Jesper began to conjure up thoughts only a desperate man could. Back at camp he had several boxes of dried milk powder. Maybe he could make up a drink that would work too, and with his new supplies from Oro Fino there was no telling what else he could dream up to keep this Shoshone child from dying. Jesper had never been married, never had children of his own. He looked down at the little brown face, realizing at seventy-one years old he had no choice but to try and become a father for the first time, no matter how long the odds.

He looked down, beginning to talk to himself out loud.

'You know, if you make it I'll have to give you a name. I'll call you . . . Jonathan Little Bear Tubbs. Jonathan was my father's name. I always liked it. That would honour your chief, and me too. By jingo, I think it sounds real good!'

Immediately after arriving back at Fort Pakston, Captain Ryder ordered a military burial for the men killed in the savage fighting at the Shoshone village. Lieutenant Trivette had counted two dead troopers with five men wounded. Much to his dismay, Ryder's count was even higher, with four killed and seven more wounded. As six flag-draped pine caskets were lowered into the rich brown earth above the Madison River, the sound of the chaplain reading over them was drowned out by the captain's own thoughts and growing fears. His loses were far higher than he ever expected. When those kind of numbers reached his superiors back at Fort Laramie, what would they think of his command decisions? A stain like that on his military record could be devastating. Those .44-.40, lever action, 16-shot Henry rifles were the cause of this disaster. But the review, when it was read, would still hold him to account for the entire action. Ryder only saw one way to redeem himself and keep his reputation as a hard-driving officer intact.

By the time the chaplain had finished the service and the company of men started back inside the log walls of the fort, Captain Ryder had already begun formulating a plan to save himself and possibly even come out a hero. If he could find the man or men who supplied the Shoshones with those Henry rifles and bring them to justice, the focus of the entire campaign could change dramatically into a stunning success. He hailed Sergeant Cleary over, the two men now standing alone, outlining his new plan. The sergeant nodded in agreement, bringing up his earlier trip into town.

'You may remember when I went to Eagle Buttes to buy supplies sometime back, I talked to a man there named R.T. Sturgis. He was the leader of the party of men that went into the mountains supposedly on a search for gold. He's also the very same man who shot Frank Jury dead. Jury was one of the two wagon traders who came here saying they wanted to trade with the Crows.'

'Yes, I remember all that. Go on.'

'The traders' whole story never made a lot of sense to me, but I didn't have time to keep track of them every day. Eventually the pair pulled out of here at night, and I never saw them again. Sturgis and Jury were the only two men who made it back out of the Tobacco Root Mountains alive as far as I know. There could be some kind of connection between them. I don't know exactly what it might be, but there's something about this whole business that says it's more than just a coincidence.'

The captain looked away, pulling at his jaw and thinking Cleary's suspicions over.

'I think it's time we took a small complement of men and rode for Eagle Buttes. This kind of Indian uprising by Standing Bear could spread to other tribes like wildfire, even though he's dead. Something like that can also take years to put down at a frightful cost of lives. I want you to choose half a dozen of your best men. I'll let Trivette take care of things here while we're gone. We'll leave tomorrow. If I have to declare martial law once we arrive to get the answers I want, I will do exactly that. I'm going to get to the bottom of this and you, Mr Cleary, are going to help me!'

NINE

Jesper Tubbs began transforming his meagre mountain camp into a nursery of sorts even though he had absolutely no knowledge or experience of taking care of a child. He'd saved the little Shoshone baby from certain death; now he meant to do everything under the sun he could to keep him alive. He's seen Shoshone women nursing and caring for their babies when visiting the village. Those scenes set him to thinking. He cut off a piece of hide from a deer skin and stitched it into a small cone shape, making a tiny incision in the bottom end. With the powdered milk he mixed thick slurry and poured it into the cone, lightly touching the baby's mouth. Baby Jonathan eagerly began sucking the milk down until the deer skin tit was completely empty. Jesper was encouraged to try other ideas.

His next attempt was a thick soup-like broth made from pounding venison into powder, adding water, and some broth he made from shooting a pair of blue grouse and boiling their meat, heart and liver in a big pot. All that went into the deer-skin 'bottle' and was sucked down with the same satisfying results.

Tubbs remembered the woven baskets Shoshone women made to hold their infants for carrying, riding and sleeping in. He gathered willow branches and fashioned a crude one of his own, folding a piece of old blanket in the bottom for padding. Each day when he began going back down to the gold ridge, he propped the baby up in it so he could keep one eye on him while he hammered away. Tubbs also decided the thin lean-to he had lived in for so long needed to be made better to keep out the wind and cold. He fashioned a better roof with rounds of bark, and lined the walls with thick grasses, also making the rock-lined fireplace out front larger to reflect more heat inside.

The little child seemed to be growing and prospering, but Jesper could not stop worrying the baby might suddenly get sick or injured in some way, needing real medical care. He was no doctor. He'd always found a way to take care of himself way back here in the mountains, but this was a different story. Oro Fino lay far away, too far if something really serious overtook his adopted son. If he brought the child into town, authorities might try to take him away, putting him into a real home. Do-gooders were everywhere, and they didn't all have badges either. The more days that successfully passed, the more determined Tubbs became that nothing and no one would get between him and his infant, who had so suddenly changed his life and given it more meaning that he'd ever imagined possible. He might be old, white-haired and physically broken down in some ways, but the man who was at first a reluctant

father, now swore only death would keep him and
Jonathan apart.

Captain Ryder and his men reached Eagle Buttes with
hard riding one week after the military funeral. He and
his cavalrymen rode down the street into town to a
growing crowd of onlookers following along on boardwalks, pointing and talking excitedly about the sudden
appearance of smartly dressed troopers. Cas Wickman
heard the commotion outside the door of his office.
Getting to his feet, he stepped outside to see what all the
excitement was about. One look at what he saw coming
down the street sent a flash of fear straight through him.
He well remembered Sergeant Cleary's visit earlier and
the probing questions he'd asked both him and Sturgis.
Now he was back with even more men. That could only
mean more trouble. Before the line of riders reached
his office, he rushed back inside, closing the door
behind him. Crossing the room, he exited out the side
door into a narrow alley, fast-stepping to R.T.'s office.

'There's trouble coming, and I mean it!' He pushed
into Sturgis's office, out of breath, staring at his boss
sitting behind his big oak desk.

'Yes, I already know about it. You just keep your
mouth shut and let me do all the talking if they show up
here. They might just be passing through on the way to
someplace else. Don't get yourself all worked up for no
reason.'

Sergeant Cleary pulled his horse to a halt in front of
the sheriff's office. 'This is it, sir. If I remember correctly the sheriff's name is Wickman.'

119

Ryder dusted off his hat before swinging down out of the saddle. 'You stay here and tell the men to rest easy for a few minutes. I'll talk to this man myself. It's Sturgis I want both of us to question, wherever he is here in town.'

Entering the office, Ryder looked around the empty room. A half-filled coffee mug sat on the desk. He walked over, testing it with his hand. Still hot. Wickman must have left only moments earlier. Two small jail cells lined the opposite wall. The captain crossed the room looking into the first one; empty. The second held a frowzy-haired man lying on a bunk, still hung over from the previous evening's losing battle with a bottle of rye whiskey. The bleary-eyed drinker looked up at the sound of Ryder's hard-soled boots crossing the floor.

'I'm looking for Sheriff Wickman. Was he just here?'

The disheveled man pulled himself upright, sitting on the edge of the bunk. Rubbing his face with both hands, he tried clearing the whiskey cobwebs from the throbbing ache in his head.

'He . . . went out that way . . . general.' The informer pointed a finger toward the side door.

'Did he say where he was going?'

'Ahhhh . . . no, but probably over to . . . Sturgis's office. That's where . . . he hangs out when he ain't . . . in here.'

'And where would that be?'

'It's . . . down the alley . . . across the street. Got a big . . . sign over the front door.'

'Thank you. I'll look for him there.'

'Ahhhh . . . if you see him . . . ask him to come back and . . . turn me loose. I need to git back to my . . . wife. She's probably wonderin' where . . . I am by now.'

'I would imagine she is, but when she sees the shape you're in you might wish you were back in here.'

Captain Ryder exited the office. Mounting up, he turned to Sergeant Cleary. 'This man Sturgis we've come to see has an office one block over from here. Wickman could be there too, but it's Sturgis I want to talk to. After a week of hard riding to get here, I want some answers from him that make sense. I'm in no mood to bandy words with him or anyone else either.'

When the cavalrymen reined their horses to a stop in front of R.T.'s office, Wickman was already standing behind the thin curtain covering the window staring outside. He instantly stepped back.

'They're here, the whole bunch of them right out front.'

'Get away from that window and sit down on the couch. And keep your mouth shut once they come inside. These soldier boys might think they're real smart, but if they had any brains they wouldn't have joined the military in the first place. Nobody's got anything on me or you, and that's the way we're going to keep it. The less I say, the less they know. They can sniff around all they want. It's not going to do them any good, and we sure as hell won't help them either.'

A loud knock on the office door ended R.T.'s comments. He put a finger to his lips, before calling out. 'Come in!'

The door opened and Captain Ryder, followed by

Sergeant Cleary, stepped into the spacious room to find Sturgis sitting behind his big desk. Wickman, over on the couch, sat stock still like a statue. Ryder's and Sturgis's eyes met as the captain walked across the room, each sizing up the other for the first time. Ryder removed his hat and leather riding gloves, stopping in front of the desk.

'I'm Captain Rutherford R. Ryder, a week out of Fort Pakston. I assume you are R.T. Sturgis?'

'You assume correctly. Excuse me for not standing. I'm still suffering physical disabilities from almost being killed by the Shoshone Indians the cavalry is supposed to be protecting all us citizens from.' R.T.'s voice had his intentional mocking ring to it.

'That is something you will no longer have to worry about, Mr Sturgis. My men and I attacked and destroyed the Shoshone village killing everyone in it, including Standing Bear himself, just weeks ago. His attack against you is exactly what brings me and my men here to Eagle Buttes. We now have complete control over the Tobacco Root Mountains, and everyone who goes into it for whatever reasons. That should be good news to you. But I have more pressing questions that need answers, and I believe you are the man who can give them to me, being the good citizen I'm sure you are.'

'And what would that be, captain?' Sturgis sat back in his chair, continuing to play his game of cat and mouse.

'The Shoshones we attacked were all armed with brand new Henry repeating rifles. Because of it I lost a number of good men and even more wounded. I had to bury those young men before riding here, and I mean to find out who supplied the Shoshone with those weapons and ammunition, if it's the last thing I do. Whoever it is, the army will bring to trial and vigorously prosecute, either to put them behind bars for twenty years, or possibly even to hang. I can assure you the death of United States cavalrymen is no small matter. A case of this magnitude will be tried in federal court, likely in Wichita, not by some local town judge. Eagle Buttes is the only town for fifty miles in any direction. Those rifles had to come from here. I will find out from who, and how they were delivered.'

Cas Wickman stiffened in his chair, mouth pulled tight as he eyed Sturgis. Cleary saw it but said nothing at that moment. Now Ryder had another ace up his sleeve, and he played it.

'Sergeant Cleary remembers two wagon traders that made the long trip to our fort sometime back. They supposedly came to trade with the Crow Indians, whose village is near us. One of those men was named Jury. I'm told you killed a man by the same name right here in town. Is that correct, Mr Sturgis?'

R.T. tried to remain cool and steady, moving only slightly in the chair and still eyeing the captain. He tossed off the question with a wave of his hand. 'Everyone here knows Jury tried to kill me in the middle of the night while I lay in bed under a doctor's care, damn near helpless. I got lucky and shot him before he could me. It was self-defence, plain and simple. Any man would do the same, even you, captain, or would you just lay there and let yourself get killed?'

Ryder didn't hesitate or answer. Instead he bored in further. 'There was another man riding with Jury when he came to our fort. Do you know what his name was?'

'I'm told that might be Delbert Hoyt.'

'And where is he now?'

'Hoyt was killed when me and my men were attacked by the Shoshone. What's left of him is likely only a pile of bones by now, someplace back in the mountains.'

'So both Jury and Hoyt rode with you and they're the same two men who came to Fort Pakston. It seems pretty obvious to me that they both worked for you, didn't they, Mr Sturgis?'

'Yes, they worked for me from time to time doing odd jobs. But they asked for some time off and I gave it to them. I didn't ask why or what for, and they didn't tell me either. They also wanted to rent one of my freight wagons for a couple of weeks. I let them for a small fee. I would imagine that's when they showed up at your place to trade with the Crows you mentioned. I got my wagon back and that was the end of it.'

'I believe I can make a pretty good guess what they had in your wagon. It was those Henry rifles. All I have to do now is find out where they got their hands on them. Someone here in this town had to have sold them to them. You have any ideas who that might be?'

R.T. tried clearing his throat, without success. Reaching for a large glass pitcher of water on his desk, he poured half a glass before slowly drinking it down, while glancing over at Wickman, who was clearly becoming more nervous by the minute.

'As I said, I don't know about any rifles. I don't even carry a weapon my own self. I'm not a violent man, captain. I'm a businessman, and a quite successful one if I do say so myself. '

Ryder suddenly turned on Cas. 'What about you, Sheriff? You're supposed to be the law around here. If there were any rifle sales that big you'd know about it, wouldn't you?'

The sheriff glanced at his boss, who still sat stone-faced, staring back at him. 'I ahhh, don't know about any Henry rifles either. I wasn't even on the trip into the mountains, when Mr Sturgis and his men were attacked. I didn't have anything to do with any of this. I swear it!'

'But you did know Jury and Hoyt, didn't you?' Ryder quickly followed up.

'Well yeah, I knew them, so what docs that prove? I know a lot of people around town.'

'What is obvious to me is that in your capacity as sheriff, you'd know about any rifle sales meant to end up in Indian hands, and especially by your two friends Jury and Hoyt. Either that or you're so incompetent that badge you're wearing is town joke.'

'He said he doesn't know,' R.T. suddenly broke in, seeing Wickman struggling to answer. 'This isn't some court of law, and you're not a prosecutor either. You can't just come riding into Eagle Buttes and treat people like they're common criminals. Who in hell do you think you are? That uniform doesn't make you God!'

'I'll tell you who I am, Mr Sturgis. I'm placing this

125

entire town under martial law by the authority vested in me by the United States Army, backed by Washington, D.C.. I'm going into every store and business in Eagle Buttes to find out who sold those rifles and who paid for them. When I learn that name, I'm going to place the person or persons responsible under arrest, and hold them to stand trial in federal court. Right now I'm ordering you and your miserable excuse for a sheriff not to try to leave town for any reason until I get those answers. If either of you do, I'll arrest you straight away and lock you up in your own jail!'

This time Sturgis held his tongue, as Ryder and Cleary exited the office, leaving both men still sitting staring at each other. Cas was clearly in a state of shock from the sudden order and threat. He hadn't killed anyone and was not part of the group of men who rode into the Tobacco Root Mountains on their ill-fated journey, yet now he was being roped into the whole murderous mess. He slowly shook his head, staring at the floor, before speaking.

'He's going to find out about those rifles for sure. Then what, R.T.? I didn't have anything to do with any of that, and you know it. I'm not going to prison or maybe stand trial for a hanging because of it. I'll tell you that right now.'

'You listen to me. First, you keep your mouth shut and do what I tell you to. Those two are just trying to put the prod on us hoping we'll break. I'm not going to do that and neither are you. Get some backbone, and stop whimpering like some snot-nosed kid.'

'But you bought those rifles right here in town. Ryder said he is going into every business until he finds out who sold them to you.'

'I don't care what he said. I ordered Weems and John Denning to keep their mouths shut about it. They know their necks are in this, too. Neither of them is going to tell Ryder a damn thing. We're all in this together, and we all have to stick together. That includes you too, and don't you forget it. Get yourself over to both of them and tell them what's going on and to keep their mouths shut good and tight. Don't let Ryder or his sergeant see you either. I'll stop all this even before it gets started. Get moving.'

R.T. watched his sheriff get up, starting for the office door. He'd always thought of Cas Wickman as the weakest link in his chain of lies. Now he was more certain of it than ever. Sturgis had disposed of Jury and Hoyt to cover his tracks. That only left one more man to guarantee he stayed in the clear. As Wickman reached for the door handle, Sturgis stopped him.

'Listen, I've got another idea. I want us to meet tonight to go over all this again in detail, but not here in my office. Ryder will probably have someone watching it and your place, too. Let's meet down at the old ferry crossing on the Feather River, about ten o'clock. Walk down so we don't have to get horses or my buggy. Be certain you're not being watched or followed, all right?'

The sheriff stopped, looking back over his shoulder. 'Why out there at that hour?'

'I just told you. Ryder and his soldier boys will be all

over town. I'm not going to give him anything to get more suspicious over than he already is. We'll get clear of all this if we just use our heads and stick together like I said. Remember, ten o'clock.'

TEN

Cas sat at his office desk in the dark with the door locked. The faint glow of a quarter moon outside coming through the window illuminated the clock face on the wall, steadily ticking away. 9:40. The walk to the river would take about twenty minutes. He got to his feet. Crossing the room, he parted the curtain on the window, looking outside. A few dark figures of men moving along the boardwalk passed heading for the saloons and gambling houses that stayed open all night long. As their footfalls faded away, he went to the door, slowly unlocking it turning the handle, but stopped for a moment. His hand went down feeling the thick, leather gun-belt on his side, and the cold steel of his .45 calibre six-gun snug in its holster. He'd never fired a shot at anyone in his life, and wasn't even sure he could, badge or not. But the feel of it was at least somewhat reassuring. Stepping outside, he locked the door behind him, starting up the street at a fast walk toward the end of town.

The walk through the coolness of night mountain air

was brisk and crowded with thoughts and questions about Captain Ryder and his order declaring martial law. R.T. Sturgis had always ruled Eagle Buttes with an iron hand. Now this cavalry captain had come riding into town and quickly changed all that. His boss was no longer in control. Since that afternoon's confrontation in R.T.'s office, Cas had begun to harbour thoughts about packing up his few personal possessions and leaving town fast without telling anyone, including Sturgis. Sturgis had always done all the thinking for him, Jury and Hoyt. He was the only one left alive out of the three. Maybe the time had come for Cas Wickman to begin making decisions on his own. The dangerous threat of trial and years spent rotting away in a federal penitentiary was enough to convince him he was right.

The silken hiss of fast-moving water in the Feather River alongside the road muffled Wickman's steps as he closed in on the remains of the old ferry crossing that had been abandoned years earlier for a newer one upstream. Behind shadowed pilings just ahead, he did not see the dark figure of a man hidden, watching, waiting, eyes straining into the night as the sheriff quick-stepped closer until he came to a stop and called out.

'R.T., you out here?'

Cas did not see the dull glint of moonlight off a rifle barrel slowly being raised, the shooter steadying the weapon on his outstretched hand against the piling for a sure kill.

'Sturgis, are you . . .'

BOOM! The sudden sound of a shot cut Wickman's call short as a red-hot bullet smashed into his chest, driving him onto his back. His hand quivered, trying to reach the pistol on his side, then fell motionless.

R.T. carefully ejected the spent cartridge from the Henry rifle, pocketing it before stepping out behind cover. Walking to Wickman's body, he jacked a fresh round into the chamber in case it was needed. Even in the dim glow of moonlight, it was clear it was not. Leaning down, he unpinned the sheriff's badge on Cas's vest, tossing it into the river. Putting the rifle down, he began the struggle, with his gimpy leg, to slowly drag the body inch by inch towards the rushing water. Panting for breath, he reached it. With one final grunt of effort, he shoved the body into the fast-moving current, watching it quickly bob away into the night.

Sturgis had finally taken care of the last man alive with any knowledge of his murderous plans to find Jesper Tubbs' golden strike. He stood a man relieved, with no troubling conscience about what he'd done or the men he'd killed doing it. Now he'd face Captain Ryder one-on-one exactly the way he'd wanted it. If only Weems and Denning kept their mouths shut he'd be in the clear for sure. Even they were never told why he'd purchased the rifles.

As promised, Ryder began his methodical questioning by going door to door up and down the street in every business in Eagle Buttes. Wickman had warned both store owners in advance of the captain's search the previous day, as ordered by Sturgis. When Ryder and Cleary walked into Denning's store they quickly noticed the pistols, shotguns and rifles displayed for sale behind the counter on the wall and also under the glass counter top. The middle-aged proprietor remained cool and steady in his denial about any knowledge of the rifles throughout Ryder's questioning, before the captain asked to see his shipping records. Denning retrieved the ledger without the slightest hesitation. After carefully reviewing them and finding nothing, the officer closed the book.

'Thank you, Mr Denning.' Ryder slid the big book back across the counter top. 'I do appreciate your cooperation in this matter. I would also ask that if you happen to hear anything pertaining to these rifles I'm inquiring about, you will not hesitate to let me know of it.'

'I will,' Denning smiled, certain he'd cleared himself of any suspicion. 'How long do you and your men plan on being here in town, captain?'

'I'm not certain just yet. It depends how quickly I can found out who was involved in supplying these rifles and also who purchased them.'

'I see,' the business owner smiled confidently, sticking out his hand. 'Good luck with your search, captain, and you too sergeant.'

Denning escorted the pair to the door. Closing it behind him, he went to the window and watched the tall man in blue and his aide stride up the street to the next store. He'd never imagined his part in the rifles purchase and sale to Sturgis would lead to something this serious. Now that it had, he wondered about the other half of the story, Sirius Weems. He was well aware Weems was a shifty-eyed, nervous little man who was always endlessly worrying about everything, even when business was good. Under the kind of questioning he was about to get from this captain, he feared Weems might break or say something that would implicate him, too. Denning's fears were not without merit.

Weems had originally tried to back out of the rifles purchase, but R.T. forced him to go through with it on the threat he'd finish off his lucrative business and close him down. Sturgis still held the deed to the property Weems was paying on each month, and had a long way to go before he owned it outright. Weems kept muttering to himself he wished he'd never gotten involved in the whole mess that had now grown even worse with the cavalry involved. Besides that, like Denning, he didn't know Sturgis meant to trade the rifles to Shoshone Indians either. Maybe he could fall back on that excuse for an alibi, if it came to that. An hour after questioning Denning, Ryder and Sergeant Cleary walked into Sirius's store to the ring of a little bell hung over the door. Weems was on a low foot stool stocking shelves, his back to the door. When he got down and turned around, the look on his face suddenly changed to one of a condemned man facing a hanging rope. At that very same moment across the street, R.T. Sturgis stood at his office window, leaning on a cane and watching the two men entering Weems' store. He said a silent prayer that the little man would keep his mouth shut.

'Mr Weems, I'm Captain Ryder, and this is Sergeant Cleary, my assistant.' The captain took his hat off, placing it on the counter and making it clear he meant to stay a while. 'I'm here to . . .'

'I don't know nuthin' about any rifles!' Weems cut him off, with a growing scowl on his face, looking from Ryder to Cleary.

The captain glanced at his sergeant, both instantly knowing they'd found the man they'd been looking for.

'I haven't asked you about any rifles. Why would you even bring that up, sir?'

'Everyone in town's talking about it . . . that's why. I'm already sick and tired of hearing it. You two go bother someone else. I got me a business to run, not waste time flapping my jaws about a lot of dumb questions I don't know nuthin' about.'

'Then you must also know I've declared martial law of the whole town, don't you? That means I have complete control over everyone in it, and the authority to question anyone I deem important to my search for these rifle sales. That also includes business records and yours, too.'

Sirius let out a breath of exasperation, squinty eyeing the captain, but did not answer this time.

'The first question I want to ask you is, do you have knowledge about where those Henry rifles either came from and who purchased them?'

'Nope,' was his one-word reply.

'You would do well to remember what I'm asking you. Anyone who withholds evidence about this will face a federal judge, and I don't mean some local politician here in town, either.'

'I said I don't know!'

'Then I'd like to see your business records for the last five months. Get them out, please.'

Sirius kept his resentful stare on the captain while reaching under the counter. Pulling up a large, flat ledger, he tossed it across the counter. 'Here, help yourself!'

Captain Ryder opened the book and began carefully scanning the first page, then the second containing the most recent entries, plus the dates and amounts of each purchase for the goods delivered. Weems' open defiance and reaction to his presence seemed the exact opposite of the carefully detailed entries and notes written in the margin of each page. The third page of the ledger was clearly missing, only a thin, jagged torn out edge remaining.

'What about this page?' Ryder stabbed a finger, looking up at the little man again.

Sirius took a quick glance. 'I spilled some coffee on it. Washed out most the ink, so I tore it out. So what?' he shrugged, proud of his quick thinking.

'Do you still have it?'

'Nope. I burned it in that pot-bellied stove behind you,' he nodded toward the big, cast-iron vessel sitting in the middle of the room.

'So, how would you know if you made a profit or loss for those weeks?'

'I don't worry none about it. I'd make it up on the next page. Business has been good, if that's any business of yours.'

Ryder's eyes went back to the ledger as Cleary leaned in beside him, also studying the figures and dates. So far Weems had an alibi for everything he'd asked, but the captain wasn't done yet. He looked back up at the little man.

'Where do you purchase your supplies from, Mr Weems?'

'What do you mean, where?'

'I mean it's obvious you sell a large variety of goods. I'm certain most of it is not made here in town. You must have to order it from someplace else and have it brought in by freight wagon.'

Weems squirmed at the question. He quickly understood what the officer was driving at. He had to think fast. 'I buy my supplies from lots of different places. What difference does that make?'

'I'll tell you what. You sell weapons along with other goods here in this store, the same way John Denning does. Your two businesses probably account for most of the weapons sold in this entire town. I see some notions on what's left of that torn out page that says you make large purchases from down in Richfield, in the valley. Isn't that so, Mr Weems?'

Sirius's jaw tightened and his lips stuck out, glaring back at the officer. This little game they were playing just turned more deadly, and he didn't like the change in odds. The Henry rifles had come from Richfield. Those notions Ryder was talking about were his way of not revealing the sales or who they were for, but that he had paid for them.

'I expect an answer, do you have one, Mr Weems?'

Ryder bored in.

'I buy some goods from down there, and other stuff from other places. Some probably come from back east or even down south. I have no way of knowing that, and neither does anyone else, including you.'

'I might not right now, but I soon will. How far away is Richfield from here?'

'I don't know ... I don't go there. It might take a freight wagon four or five days to get up here. I never asked.'

'It's a little hard to believe you don't know anything about businesses you purchase most of your goods from. Is that what you're telling me?'

Sirius knew what was coming. Ryder meant to send riders all the way down to Richfield to get those answers. Straightening up behind the counter, he'd had enough.

'I'm tired of answering all these damn foolish questions. Why don't you go ask someone else? I got better things to do right here in my store. I've told you all I know. I ain't got time to play any more games with you two.'

'Games, you say? I can assure you this isn't any game, Mr Weems. We're talking about the death of valiant United States cavalrymen and who supplied the rifles that killed them. When I find out who was involved in all this, you have my promise I'll see them in federal prison and keep them there for the rest of their miserable lives!'

The captain turned to Sergeant Cleary, after he'd calmed himself down. 'Do you have a penknife, sergeant?'

'I do, sir.' He reached into his pocket and retrieved the small, fold-up blade, handing it to Ryder, who carefully cut out the thin strip of the torn out page before folding it up and putting it in his tunic.

'I want you to take two men with fast horses and ride for Richfield. Find out who down there shipped those Henry rifles up here and to who. Get a written statement on the date, amount of money paid, and how many rifles and ammunition boxes were delivered. And tell whatever business you find they'll likely be called for federal trial to back up the paperwork. I'll notify them of that date when I hear from command. Get back up soon as possible with all this.'

'Yes, sir.' Cleary saluted, quickly turning on his heels and striding out of the Weems store. Ryder turned back to Weems with one last order for him.

'Don't you try to leave town for any reason. I'll post men at roads leading in and out of here to be certain my orders are carried out. Do I make myself clear, Mr Weems?'

Sirius tried to hide the fear beginning to well up inside him with a bold show of bravado. 'What makes you think I'd want to leave town? I got no reason to do that. You go ahead and run all over the country like a chicken with its head cut off. I'll just sit back and watch it.'

'I'm glad to hear that Mr Weems. When Sergeant Cleary gets back from Richfield, you and I are going to have another long talk about this matter. In the meantime, I would suggest you seriously begin thinking about cooperating with me, or whether you're ready to spend the rest of your life in a federal penitentiary. Believe me when I tell you, I am the man who can put you there.'

The captain left the store with Weems standing there, sweat beginning to run down his thin, unshaven face. He scratched his head, knowing what news the sergeant would bring back from Richfield. He also made the quick decision he wasn't going to prison because of what R.T. Sturgis forced him to do. He had to talk to Sturgis, and fast. Late that afternoon he locked up the store early. Pulling down the shades over the front windows, he peeked outside to be sure no blue coats were watching the store. Stepping out, he locked up and started across the street.

R.T. was asleep in his big padded chair when Sirius pushed through the door into his office without even knocking. Sturgis grunted awake at the commotion as Weems came up to the desk. 'What are you doing here at this hour?' R.T. scowled at being woken up. 'I told you not to come over here during daylight.' He pulled himself full up in the chair.

'What I'm doin' is trying to keep from being measured for a hangman's rope, that's what. And all of it is because of those damn rifles you insisted on me buying for you!'

'I told both you and Denning to keep your mouths shut and everything would be all right, didn't I?'

'Well, that ain't working out so well. That captain went through my books this afternoon and sent his men down to Richfield to find out who sold the rifles to me and Denning. When he gets back, Ryder is going to have the answer, so you better start coming up with something else, and I mean real quick. I'll tell you right now, I ain't going to rot in some prison because of those rifles of yours. I didn't even know you were going to trade them to the Shoshones, or I'd never bought them in the first place!'

Sturgis slowly got to his feet. Grabbing his cane, he walked slowly across the room and looked out the front window, his mind spinning at the sudden news. After a long pause he spoke without turning around. 'You'd better go back to your place while I think all this over. Stay there until I send for you. Don't come running back over here. One of those soldier boys might see you, or even Ryder himself. He's trying to put the prod on us to see if anyone will break and talk. We cannot let that happen. You, me and Denning have to keep our mouths shut, period. You tell Denning that, too. I'll get back to you when I come up with something.'

'Like what? Ryder wants all three of us hung or in prison. He ain't gonna' stop until he gets all the answers. He's like a dog gnawing on a bone!'

'Just calm yourself down for a minute. I've already had one idea. I can tell Ryder I sold the rifles to Jury and Hoyt, and didn't know what they were going to do with them. Neither one is around to say any different are they?'

Weems thought for a moment. 'Ahh . . . that might work, but you better tell Cas what's going on too, so he don't say something wrong.'

'Yes, I'll do that when I see him. He said something about taking a few days off to go see his sister down south. Now get out of here and do what I said. We'll talk again when things cool down.'

Weems had barely gotten back inside his store when Sturgis crossed the room, going to his safe. Opening it, he lifted out the large, black tray and brought it to his desk. Then he began taking out row after row of neatly wrapped one hundred dollar bills, placing them in a big leather satchel. He'd promised Weems he'd be working on their problem all right, and that's exactly what he was doing. The news that Captain Ryder had sent his men to ride for Richfield suddenly changed everything. That was getting too close for comfort. It was time for him to flee Eagle Buttes, in the middle of the night, and take his over one hundred thousand dollars with him. With that kind of money he could go anywhere he wanted, even back east to some big city where he could change his name and no one would ever find him. Maybe he might even leave the country and live in Mexico. He could live like a king down there for the rest of his life. Weems was right about one thing; once Ryder got his hands on those shipping records, he, Sirius and Denning would all be arrested, and Weems would be the first to break trying to save himself. Before closing the bulging money bag, he retrieved a pistol from the top drawer of the desk, placing it atop all the bills. Nothing was going to stop R.T. Sturgis from leaving town. He sat back down at his desk, placing both hands on top of the leather satchel, satisfied with his new plans. All he needed now was for night to fall.

*

The lights in town finally burned low as the stores closed, and stars came out in the night sky burning icy white like a billion, blazing diamonds as night finally came. Sometime later, down at the livery stable, the owner, Mervin Johns, woke to the constant knocking on the door of his small house, which was part of the stable complex. Still half asleep, Johns came to the door, opening it just far enough to peek outside. 'Who is it?' he grumbled, until he heard R.T.'s voice.

'I need for you to get my horse and buggy ready. There's a one hundred dollar bill waiting for you when you do.'

Johns scratched his head, trying to wake up and make some sense of the strange request. 'You want to ride out now?' he finally got out the words.

'I do, and I want it as fast as you can get it done. Who else is going to pay you one hundred dollars for twenty minutes' work!'

Half an hour later, bundled up against the chill night air, Sturgis whipped the horse ahead into the night, wheels spinning, leaving the sleeping shadows of Eagle Buttes behind. A grim smile played across his whiskered face. His new plan was working perfectly. By dawn he'd be miles away, in a week clean out of the territory. The smile didn't last long. Rounding a bend in the road minutes later, he had to haul back on the reins, braking the buggy to a sudden stop. A small, campfire burning next to the road revealed a young cavalry soldier raising his hand, stepping out into the road.

'What's all this about?' Sturgis called out as the blue coat came up to him.

'I'm sorry sir, but no one can leave town. Captain Ryder's orders. You'll have to turn around.'

'Listen to me, young man. I'm on an important business trip that cannot wait. I have no other choice. Thousands of dollars are hanging in the balance. This order has nothing to do with me, I'm sure this captain of yours will understand that. You do, don't you?'

'I don't sir. That captain says no one leaves for any reason. That's his direct orders. If I disobeyed, I'd end up in the brig, or worse.'

'I'm telling you I cannot wait. Don't you understand that? I have to leave and now, not when this captain of yours decides it's all right with some fool order that has nothing to do with me.'

The flickering firelight played across R.T.'s reddening face as his exasperation boiled to the surface. He wasn't going to let some kid in an ill-fitting uniform stop him now. He took in a deep breath, trying to contain his growing anger with one last try.

'All right, young man. Tell you what I'm willing to do to make things right.' He unsnapped the locks on the satchel reaching in. 'Here's a fifty dollar bill with your name on it if you just forget you ever saw me drive by. No one will know you took it, and you'll have three months' pay in your pocket for five minutes work. Now, does that help your conscience any?' He temptingly waved the bill in front of the young man's face.

'I . . . can't do that sir. I'm sorry.'

Sturgis stared back hard, growing more desperate by the second. 'All right, how about one hundred?' He pulled another bill from its wrapper, pushing it toward the trooper.

Private Douglas Miles slowly shook his head with a weak smile. 'I'll turn your horse around so you can head back to town. Anyone who wants to give me that kind of money ought to talk to Captain Ryder first.'

'Don't touch that horse,' Sturgis shouted, his hand reaching back into the leather case. 'I'm warning you. Step aside. I'm going through!'

Miles ignored the threat, grabbing the horse's bit and starting to lead him around, when a single, thundering pistol shot rang out and the young trooper fell face first to the ground. He moaned, struggling for a moment to try to roll over, then went limp. Sturgis instantly whipped the horse forwards, the buggy wheel careening over the trooper's body, but Private Douglas Miles was beyond any more earthly pain.

R.T.'s streaking buggy was barely an hour away from the site of Miles' murder, when a second trooper from town rode up to the road block to replace the young man for his midnight watch. Even in the fading glow of an unkempt fire, the rider could see the prostrate form of Miles laying face down in the road. Yanking his horse to a stop, he leaped from the saddle, kneeling next to Miles. Rolling him over, he saw the neat, round bullet hole in his neck oozing blood, soaking his shirt and jacket in red. Getting to his feet, the cavalryman dragged the body off the road, covering it with the blanket Miles had used to keep warm by the fire. Mounting back up, the trooper kicked his horse hard back toward town and the cavalry camp at the far end.

Along the winding road following the twisting course of the Feather River, Sturgis whipped his horse dangerously on for even more speed. Icy wind biting at his face couldn't keep back the hot sweat of fear running down his face. All his carefully laid plans had collapsed, forcing him to run for his life. He knew doing so meant an instant admission he was guilty of murder, now made worse by the killing of the young guard. Sturgis was never a man to kid himself. He wasn't about to start now with his life hanging in the balance. He had to get away as fast and far as possible, vowing not to be taken alive if it came to that. No one was going to slip a thick rope around his neck while a crowd of curious onlookers gathered like a Sunday picnic, wondering what death looked like twisting and kicking from a hanging scaffold. White flecks of sweat began coating the horse's chest and shoulders as it ran headlong into the night, feeling the constant bite of R.T.'s whip slashing its back.

In Eagle Buttes, the sleeping cavalry camp suddenly came alive, with Captain Ryder running from tent to tent, shouting orders to get up and prepare to ride, while he buttoned his tunic. Sergeant Cleary was already waiting for him when he returned to his tent.

'Make it clear to all the men I want whoever killed Private Miles taken alive. I do not want him shot for any reason. When we catch up to him, I'm going to personally hang that bastard myself. Get everyone mounted up. We've got some catching up to do!'

ELEVEN

The line of fast-riding cavalrymen reached the check-point, stopping only long enough for Ryder to order two troopers to take Miles' body back to town, roped over his horse. One of the men pointed to fresh imprints of wheel tracks in bloody dirt. 'Look captain, the last thing to pass through here was a wagon, not a man on horseback.'

Ryder looked over at Cleary. Both men came to the same conclusion at the same instant. 'Only R.T. Sturgis uses a wagon to travel,' Ryder intoned. 'Let's get after him!'

Miles ahead in the dark, Sturgis continued driving like a man possessed, abandoning any thought of safety on the narrow, winding river road. The buggy danced and skidded around one sharp turn after another, wheels spinning only inches away from going over the steep drop off into the swirling waters two hundred feet below. Every few minutes he would twist in the seat, looking back into murky shadows to be certain no one was following him. Satisfied he was still running alone, he went back to the whip, forcing the tiring horse to keep up its killing pace.

After a second hour of running he considered stopping to rest the horse and himself, before quickly abandoning the idea, cracking the whip over the animal's back into a steady run again. Someone might be gaining on him. Surely by now they'd found the body of the young trooper at the checkpoint. He had to keep running like the devil himself was after him. He was beyond realizing it was the devil at the reins driving his own buggy.

Finally the long night of fear began to brighten when the first hint of dawn outlined the black silhouette of rocky ridges high above the canyon road. R.T. wiped hot sweat off his face with the back of his gloved hand. He'd run many miles alone and began, at last, to feel he had to be in the clear. But just one turn behind the wildly careening buggy, Captain Ryder and his sergeant saw the first whip of dust disappearing around a bend in the road just ahead, causing Ryder to shout.

'That's got to be him . . . we've got him now!'

The buggy came out of the turn onto a long straightaway. Sturgis checked behind him for the tenth time that night. His eyes suddenly narrowed, the hair on the back of his neck tingling in fear, feeling like an army of ants crawling for his scalp. It looked like riders coming fast. If it was, it could only be the cavalry led by the man he'd grown to hate with a vengeance for disrupting all his carefully laid plans, forcing him to flee like this. He brought the whip down harder, screaming at the horse, before turning again to be certain tired eyes weren't

147

playing tricks on him. Now he could make out blue-clad uniforms, the long line of riders gaining ground on him. His hand grabbed for the bulging leather satchel on the seat next to him. Unsnapping the locks, he reached in, still holding the reins in one hand, and pulling up a six-gun. Swinging his arm over the seat, he pulled the trigger, firing wildly behind him and emptying the revolver.

Captain Ryder leaned low in the saddle, yelling at the men behind him. 'Don't shoot. I want him alive!'

R.T. struggled trying to reload the pistol with one hand, keeping his eyes on the road ahead at the same time. The cavalry was thundering closer. He could hear their horses eating up the distance on the fleeing buggy, yard by precious yard. Cartridges spilled from the box onto the seat. He tried scooping them up, as the buggy wove wildly, wheels spinning, from one side of the road to the other. The outside wheel skidded over the low berm, instantly spilling horse, buggy and Sturgis out into space and falling all the way down into deep, black pools of the current-laced waters with a tremendous splash.

Ryder and Cleary yanked their horses to a sudden stop. Leaping down, Ryder shouted for his men to follow him, scrambling down the steep drop-off to the river bank below. Somehow Sturgis had miraculously survived the fall and came thrashing back up to the surface, struggling for air and spitting icy water. His heavy coat, clothes and boots began soaking up water, trying to drag him back down again. The money satchel! He saw it bobbing on the surface just feet away.

He lunged for it, as Sergeant Cleary whirled a lasso over his head, sending out the loop to drop almost atop the struggling man.

'Grab the rope!' Cleary shouted, while Sturgis floundered, looking at the money bag, then the rope floating even closer.

'Sturgis, grab that damn rope and save yourself!' Ryder screamed, seeing the drowning man wild-eyed with fear and indecision.

R.T. made one final lunge with his last ounce of strength. Gripping the leather satchel in his hand, he slowly sank out of sight in the dark water. This time he did not resurface. The captain and Cleary stood on the bank, out of breath, incredulous at what they'd just witnessed.

'I had the rope right in front of him,' the sergeant shook his head. 'All he had to do was grab it. . . .'

For several long seconds neither man spoke again, stunned to silence. Finally, Captain Ryder took in a long, deep breath. 'I guess greed, money and murder are more powerful than the will to live. I would not have believed any man could do something like this if I hadn't seen it with my own eyes. It's a lesson to remember how the twisted mind of an unrepentant killer works. If nothing else, he saved the hangman a job. The Feather River owns R.T. Sturgis now, and whatever money he had in that bag. I don't think she's going to give either of them up very soon.'

Both Sirius Weems and John Denning admitted their guilt at the federal trail held in Leavenworth, Kansas, three months later. Each man was sentenced to ten years in prison, both finally given parole after serving seven years of forced, hard labour. Denning was first to make it back to Eagle Buttes upon his release. He had no money to try and go back into business again and left town months later, never to be seen or heard from again. Sirius Weems left the federal penitentiary three days after Denning, a broken shell of a man. Back-breaking labour had nearly crippled the little man. He hobbled, bent over in excruciating pain, a pathetic figure of skin and bones. He also headed back to Eagle Buttes. The only thing that kept him alive through all those years of suffering was his never-ending cantankerous attitude about everything, and everyone, every single day until his release.

People around town barely recognized him and the stigma of his part in the sale of the Henry rifles and their transfer to the Shoshone Indians slowly faded away. He went to work, taking any menial job he could find; cleaning horse stables, sweeping up the town's many saloons and emptying spittoons. Eventually he even landed a job clerking in a small store. Three years after his return, he'd saved enough money to open his own small, grocery store at the edge of town. The one item he refused to stock or sell was guns of any kind.

Captain Ryder was promoted to lieutenant colonel for his successful campaign against the Shoshone Indians, and for bringing to trial Weems and Denning, plus uncovering the ring leader of the whole rifle scheme, R.T. Sturgis. The mastermind was dead, and for that he still had lingering regrets. He'd wanted more than anything else to see Sturgis hung. He was reassigned to Arizona Territory, where the Apache Indians were running wild and refusing to be disarmed or forced onto reservations. Sergeant Cleary was also promoted to master sergeant, but stayed on at Fort Pakston.

The reluctant surrogate father Jesper Tubbs successfully raised the Shoshone baby he'd saved from certain death into a young, healthy teenager. Both still lived in the hidden camp deep in the Tobacco Root Mountains, working the gold site that had made Tubbs a rich man by then. He'd take his young son into Oro Fino with him each time he had more ore to be processed. He wanted Jonathan to get a look at what civilization looked like, small as it was. He knew this was the world he'd eventually have to face when he was gone. Jesper bought his 'son', his first horse in town, a paint pony with splashes of brown and white. When they rode out, the young man sat proudly in his new saddle as people stopped to watch the strange pair pass. Some wondered out loud if Tubbs had taken a Shoshone wife. Jesper always kept that personal part of his life to himself.

The years were catching up with Jesper and he was well aware of it. His growing bank account was registered in both his and Jonathan's name. He'd insisted on it from the start. He was in his early eighties and knew the day was coming when his 'son' would have to have access to all that money. He hated the thought of having to move into Oro Fino, but now felt he had no other choice. Another long winter passed before the pair finally left their mountain home and Tubbs bought a modest house in town. The culture shock for Jonathan was overwhelming, as Jesper knew it would be. The old prospector retold the tale of how he'd found the little baby in the destroyed Shoshone village, and that the Bighorn gold strike would make him a wealthy man when he grew to adulthood. And he continually told the young teenager not all white people were like the cavalry that had slaughtered his people, and he would have to learn to live with them in this new world of theirs when he was gone. Tubbs took Jonathan to the local school, asking the teacher, Mrs Anderson, to enrol him in class for the education he knew he would need. School barely lasted two weeks. The other boys taunted the strange kid with dark skin and long black hair down to his shoulders. They called him 'Indian boy', and 'Little chief', leading to endless fist fights out behind the school house, most of which Jonathan won, even though he was accused of starting them. Mrs Anderson finally gave up, sending a note home saying it was best Jonathan did not return to school. He was too big a distraction for the other children and a troublemaker to boot. Besides that, she suggested it was a waste of time trying to teach him anything at all because of his stubborn refusal to learn, clinging to his own language and heritage.

Jesper passed away on his son's fifteenth birthday, leaving the young man alone in the house with only troubling memories. He told no one of his father's passing. Instead, in the black of night, he tightly wrapped the old man's body in a blanket, roping it over his mule Jenny and riding deep into the forest that had once been their happy home. At dawn he found an ancient pine with a lightning-burned hollow under spreading roots. He interned the body there, covering it first with branches and limbs, then heavy stones, as was the burial rights of his people. Back in town the next day, he sat in the silent house staring at the walls, trying to decide what to do now. He had no father to point the way any more. The only real home he'd ever felt at ease with was in the mountain camp he and Jesper had shared all those years, with the man he'd slowly come to love. That afternoon he pulled down the shades and locked the front door, saddling up for the long ride back into the Tobacco Root Mountains. He was going 'home'.

Jonathan refurbished the old campsite, cutting enough firewood for a long stay. Then he went to work on the bark-walled hut, making it wind- and rainproof. Days passed while he hunted deer for meat, hanging the quarters in the cool mountain air to cure. From time to time he even went down to the golden ledge and did some work with an axe and heavy hammer. Jesper had told him that gold was the key to anything he might want to do in the future, sternly warning him never to reveal its location to anyone. The familiar healing caress of the mountains had a calming effect on the young man. He began to feel alive again for the first time. Later that summer, he felt the urge to make the long day's journey to the site of the old Indian village where he was born. Some powerful force drew him back. He didn't know why, concluding it must be the spirit of his people.

He reached it late that afternoon. Riding out of thick timber, the once lively horse meadow was overgrown in tall grass and weeds. Urging his horse into it heading for the village, he looked down to see the whitened bones and skulls of the fleet horses his people had once ridden on to victory. Reaching the village flat, no teepee poles remained standing. Winter snows, winds and cavalry torches had brought them all down long ago. The scattering of bones and skulls he saw now were not those of horses. The dim outline of a few fire pits were all that remained to show a vibrant, living community of proud men, dark-haired women and playing children had once lived here. Jonathan eased down off his horse, slowly walking through the site. Stooping, he picked up a weather-worn rifle cartridge from the battle. Could it have been the one that killed his father or mother? He tried putting the grisly thought out of his mind, quickly tossing it away. Reaching the end of the flat, he stood looking at the peaceful valley ringed in by tall, arrow-topped pines. Little wonder Standing Bear had chosen it for his summer camp.

As late afternoon shadows began creeping out from the pines toward the village site, Jonathan suddenly felt a strange, foreboding telling him to leave this place of death. He sensed evil spirits hidden in those long, shadowy fingers were reaching out to engulf him, too. Quickly saddling up, he kicked his paint pony back across the meadow at a run and flashing into thick timber, vowing never to return to this place ever again.

The young man spent the remainder of that summer living in the mountain camp, thinking about all he'd learned and everything Jesper had told him about his own life and his place in a white man's world that still seemed so strange and foreign to him. His own people were either dead or scattered far and wide on reservations, living like sheep in bare log cabins and eating tainted beef given them by white agents. There was no place in that world for him to go. His choices seemed few. He could either hide out in the mountains the rest of his life or ride back to civilization and try to change the direction of his life in a white man's world. When the first chilly nights of fall put a thin skim of ice on the camp water bucket, he'd made up his mind. Closing down camp, Jonathan gathered his few personal possessions and the ore he'd gotten, saying goodbye to the safety and serenity that had harboured him all that summer. Oro Fino and the house Jesper bought for both of them lay a full week's ride away. It was time to go back and face the world he'd shunned for so long. He would try with all his might to embrace it and make his father proud of him. The results of his efforts in the weeks and months ahead would be something no one could have imagined or dreamed possible, least of all Jonathan himself.

Reaching town, he stabled his horse and opened up the musty-smelling house and windows, clearing out the cobwebs and dust. While fresh air whisked away the past, he walked down to Oro Fino's one and only bank, the Oro Fino Mercantile. At the tellers' cage the clerk, Mrs Hattie Springfield, looked wide-eyed at her new customer's darkly tanned faced and long black hair. Her voice caught in her throat. 'Can . . . I . . . help you

155

with . . . something?'

'I want to know how much money I have in here?'

She turned, hand to her mouth, calling for the bank manager sitting at his desk behind her. 'Mr Preston . . . this . . . gentleman has a question for you.'

Anthony Preston looked up through wire-rimmed glasses, quickly recognizing the young man. Getting to his feet, he came to the tellers' cage. 'Well, hello Jonathan. It's nice to see you again. It's been quite a while since I have. Come in and I'll see if I have an answer for you.'

Preston unlocked the counter door, ushering the young man inside and motioning him to a chair opposite his desk. 'I haven't seen your father either for quite a while. Where have you two been keeping yourselves?'

'My father died a long time ago,' Jonathan answered without any show of emotion.

'Died? Oh, I'm so sorry to hear that. I knew your father to be a good man, but I never read about his passing in the paper. It must have been a private affair.'

'I buried him in the Shoshone way.'

The strange answer left Preston speechless, wondering for several seconds if he should pursue the meaning further. He decided not to.

'Well, Jonathan, I'm sure he went on to his just rewards. I knew him to be a decent man who kept to himself, and of course you. Let me change the subject. You wanted to ask me about what?'

'How much American money did my father leave in here?'

'How much? I'll have to get out the ledger to give

you an exact figure. You are the sole possessor of those funds now, but I guess you already know that. Give me a minute and I'll be right back.'

The bank manager got up from the desk, while Jonathan glanced around the strange room with its smell of old paper and stale tobacco. Back at his desk, Preston sat opening the big book. Adjusting his glasses, he ran a finger down customers' names until coming to a stop.

'Ah, here it is. Your father left you . . . twenty-eight thousand, four hundred and twelve dollars and thirty-one cents. A very tidy sum to be sure. He did right well by you and him. I just hope you don't want to draw it all out, now he's no longer with us?'

'No, I want enough to go to school.'

'School, where would you do that?'

'Here with Mrs Anderson. I'll pay her to teach me how to read and write American.'

Preston sat back in his chair, nodding his head in approval. 'That's an admirable goal, Jonathan. I know your father would be very proud to know you mean to do so. I must congratulate you myself, and I'm sure other people in town would do the same, too.'

Although Mrs Anderson had once given up on teaching a younger Jonathan anything, she now saw the real desire in his eyes to learn lessons he'd previously shunned. Over the next two years she tutored her teenage charge, finding him to be a fast and eager learner who was especially good at English and mathematics. As he reached his eighteenth birthday, he purchased four new undeveloped lots for sale at the end of town, selling all four before the year was out to newcomers who were arriving in a steadily growing Oro Fino. By his twentieth birthday the tall, handsome man with long black hair down to his shoulders dressed like a businessman with the exception of high-heeled cowboy boots and his always present wide-brimmed Stetson hat.

People in town began to admire the tall Shoshone for his soft spoken words and honest business dealings. Many of the original prejudices against him and Indians in general began to fade away. When Montana became a territory in 1864, business friends enthusiastically encouraged Jonathan to run for the legislature. At first he resisted the suggestions he had any chance to win with no experience in such a position. Eventually their insistence won him over. He threw his Stetson in the ring and won, much to his own surprise, becoming the only duly elected Native American in the entire nation to do so.

In his new and powerful position he lobbied tirelessly for new laws to help free his people from the depredations forced upon them by reservation life, winning many battles previously thought impossible. During his many tours of reservations, he met a young, beautiful Shoshone woman named Kimama Blue Flower, who also fought in her own way to help their people. They were an instant match of wills and goals. Jonathan asked for her hand in marriage just months later and she agreed. They were married with a white man's bible, but in an outdoor setting under tall pines befitting both their boundless love of nature, the very same one their Shoshone ancestors had always cherished and fought to keep free.

For all his growing fame and prestige, Jonathan kept one secret part of his life only to himself and Kimama. Once every year in the spring, he would leave the ranch they were building outside Oro Fino, saddling up his horse and two pack mules to disappear back into the Tobacco Root Mountains where he was raised. Early in their marriage before they had children, he would take Kimama with him. After his Little Wolf was born, then a daughter Grey Dove, the following year, he rode alone back to the old camp above the golden ledge his father found so many years earlier. When he returned home weeks later, the mules were unloaded with their heavy canvas sacks containing ore to be further processed in the town stamp mill, furthering his family's wealth.

Jonathan Little Bear Tubbs' life had taken a strange, twisting course unlike any other man. Strong spirits always seemed to guide and protect him. His certain death from starvation was prevented by an elderly white prospector who had never had a child of him own, yet struggled with all he had in him to save a helpless Shoshone baby. Jonathan's deep emotional debt to his surrogate father never left his thoughts. It motivated him to engage in a culture previously hostile to him and his people, yet triumph in it as even few whites ever could.

On those long, lonely rides deep into the Tobacco Root Mountains each spring he could feel the full spirit of Jesper Tubbs riding with him, a smile on his whiskered face, nodding approval that his son was following in his footsteps. The secret of Bighorn Gold would forever be kept from the greed and prying eyes of men who had killed and been killed trying to find it. Many years later Jonathan's adult son and daughter would both carry on that secret when their father's spirit rode with them, too. Even today, men still talk about and wonder if the mysterious tale of a gold strike hidden somewhere deep in the Tobacco Root Mountains really exists at all. Or is it just another Shoshone myth lost in time and endless telling? It's best none ever know that answer for sure.

whiskered face, nodding approval that his son was following in his footsteps. The secret of Bighorn Gold would forever be kept from the greed and prying eyes of men who had killed and been killed trying to find it. Many years later Jonathan's adult son and daughter would both carry on that secret when their father's spirit rode with them, too. Even today, men still talk about and wonder if the mysterious tale of a gold strike hidden somewhere deep in the Tobacco Root Mountains really exists at all. Or is it just another Shoshone myth lost in time and endless telling? It's best none ever know that answer for sure.

same one their Shoshone ancestors had always cherished and fought to keep free.

For all his growing fame and prestige, Jonathan kept one secret part of his life only to himself and Kimama. Once every year in the spring, he would leave the ranch they were building outside Oro Fino, saddling up his horse and two pack mules to disappear back into the Tobacco Root Mountains where he was raised. Early in their marriage before they had children, he would take Kimama with him. After his Little Wolf was born, then a daughter Grey Dove, the following year, he rode alone back to the old camp above the golden ledge his father found so many years earlier. When he returned home weeks later, the mules were unloaded with their heavy canvas sacks containing ore to be further processed in the town stamp mill, furthering his family's wealth.

Jonathan Little Bear Tubbs' life had taken a strange, twisting course unlike any other man. Strong spirits always seemed to guide and protect him. His certain death from starvation was prevented by an elderly white prospector who had never had a child of him own, yet struggled with all he had in him to save a helpless Shoshone baby. Jonathan's deep emotional debt to his surrogate father never left his thoughts. It motivated him to engage in a culture previously hostile to him and his people, yet triumph in it as even few whites ever could.

On those long, lonely rides deep into the Tobacco Root Mountains each spring he could feel the full spirit of Jesper Tubbs riding with him, a smile on his